# SHOT THROUGH
# THE TART

## APPLE ORCHARD COZY MYSTERY BOOK 7

### CHELSEA THOMAS

Big +
LITTLE
PRESS

*To Peekskill*
*For introducing us to our inner artist.*

# TURTLE TUMULT

*T*his story begins on a Thursday night in late March. People say the month comes in like a lion and goes out like a lamb, but that March was the meanest, rainiest lamb I'd ever met.

That particular Thursday, I'd pulled on my galoshes and raincoat and trudged through the muddy streets to the nicest restaurant in our small town, *Peter's Land and Sea.* Despite the precipitation and the lingering cold, I was in a good mood. Maybe because I was headed to dinner with Germany Turtle.

Germany was not a typical Pine Grove resident. On a scale of one to weird, he was an eleven. But he was also my boyfriend of a few months, and I couldn't wait to see him. Germany had a way of making me feel completely at ease, like even if I had milk spewing out of my nose Germany would think I looked pretty and graceful.

I shuffled into *Peter's* and shook myself off like a wet dog, then hung my raincoat on the rack in the entryway. I saw Germany, waiting at our favorite table across the room. He was wearing a crisp white shirt with a polka-dotted bowtie. Kind of hot, in a weird way.

Germany stood when I approached. "Chelsea." He opened his arms wide and I gave him a hug. "Your eyes are as radiant as all the stars in the sky. Yet it is your intellect, perseverance, and intelligence I admire most about you."

I laughed. "You look hot in a bowtie. That's the only reason I agreed to be your girlfriend."

Germany wrinkled his eyebrows. "Oh. I see. You've objectified me and my bowtie. I sense you are merely making a joke but I can't help but feel damaged by your remark."

I shook my head. "Oh, come on, Germany. You think we're only dating because I like the way you look in a bowtie?"

Germany perked up. "Got you. See? I can joke around. That time, I was pretending to be offended after you pretended to objectify me."

I smiled. "Nice job, Germany. You got me." Sometimes dating Germany was like dating an alien. But an alien with a nice smile and good manners.

Germany pulled out my chair and I sat. My former fiancé, Mike, had not been big on manners. He'd always said that holding doors or pulling out chairs was misogynist, like it implied that women couldn't open doors on their own. I'd accepted his theory and even respected it. But let me tell you, when Germany opened a door for me, I felt like a queen. And I liked it.

As I scooted in toward the table, I had no idea Pine Grove's most notorious resident would be murdered that night. So I grinned at Germany, dwelling in the flush of a new crush.

A few seconds after Germany and I sat, a middle-aged

waiter approached with his hands behind his back. The waiter was bald with a goatee. He had a little earring in his left ear and he wore a big smile as he approached. He toddled slowly toward us, like a limping penguin.

"Greetings. Welcome to *Peter's Land and Sea.* Have you dined with us before?"

Germany and I exchanged a confused look. "We're here all the time. This is our second favorite restaurant in town. You must be new here," I said, and reached out my hand for a handshake. "I'm Chelsea. This is my boyfriend, Germany."

The man smiled but did not shake my hand. "Great to meet you. I'm Petey's uncle, Jefferson Nebraska. I grew up in Pine Grove. Left ten, fifteen years ago. Got on my motorcycle and rode all the way across the country, then back, then back again. Everybody told me not to go, 'cuz I got in an accident once when I was a teenager, messed up this leg bad. But I'm glad I didn't listen. Traveling the country was a beautiful thing."

Germany smiled. "But now you're back in Pine Grove once more?"

Jefferson nodded. "I heard my nephew opened the hottest new restaurant in town. My background's in the service and hospitality industries. Came over to help him out. Proud uncle. That's what my T-shirt would say if I weren't wearing this dapper uniform."

"If you're from Pine Grove, you might know my aunt," I said. "Miss May?"

Jefferson slapped his thigh. "Miss May. Hold on, are you Chelsea Thomas? You're practically royalty in this town. That orchard is legendary. I knew Miss May when I was a kid. Went apple-picking up there. Loved every second. One time, ate so many apples I was sick for a week. OK, not a week. At least a day." Jefferson threw back his head and laughed.

Germany and I laughed. Jefferson, like his nephew Petey, had a happy glimmer in his eye and his laughter was boisterous and strange. We all made small talk for one or two more minutes, then Germany and I both ordered a big bowl of butternut squash soup with a grilled cheese to share.

Germany and I chatted while we waited for our food. Then the grilled cheese came. It was incredible. Three kinds of local, artisan cheese on a fresh-baked loaf of sourdough. It crunched, then oozed, then crunched, then oozed, every time I took a bite. My whole body felt warm when I swallowed. Petey had a knack for elevating simple dishes to make them even more savory and delightful. He had gained a reputation for the best grilled cheese in the area and he deserved it. Even if that status made his mentor, my friend Teeny, a little jealous.

But this story isn't about grilled cheese. Maybe you wish it was. But what it's really about is that murder I mentioned. Remember, the death of Pine Grove's most notorious resident? OK, so that guy didn't technically die until the next day. But the drama began during my meal of grilled cheese and butternut squash soup with Germany Turtle.

As it happened, Germany was tied up in the middle of all that drama. He'd been distracted during dinner, even though he didn't want to admit it.

"You seem distracted," I said. "What's going on?"

Germany shook his head. "Nothing. It's fine."

Germany had been working as the director of the new play at the community theater. I knew the job had been stressing him out, even if he tried not to talk about it. "Did something happen at rehearsal tonight?"

"I don't want to complain," he said. "I just want to keep moving forward."

"Complaining usually makes me feel better. Come on. Talk to me."

Germany sighed. "It's just... We have our first show tomorrow night and nothing is going well. Adam doesn't know his lines. He's supposed to be this great actor, but he keeps messing up. So that's concerning me."

I shook my head. "That's so surprising. That guy never shuts up about the big roles he had on Broadway when he was younger."

Germany shrugged. "I know. But he's not professional. He makes everything more difficult. I hate to admit it, we got into a bit of a yelling match earlier today. I scolded Adam for forgetting his lines. He scolded me for being a dictator, not a director. I insulted his work ethic. It wasn't good. And the whole love triangle among Adam, his wife Dorothy, and his costar Zambia isn't helping."

Zambia was a beautiful woman originally from the Caribbean. She was graceful, elegant and poised.

Adam's wife, Dorothy, was also beautiful, but in a cold, intimidating way. Dorothy had a reputation for being possessive and jealous. Zambia and Adam were supposed to share a kiss on stage, and it displeased Dorothy.

"Is Dorothy interfering in rehearsal?"

Germany sighed. "She sits in the back of the theater the entire time. Apparently she wants to make sure Adam doesn't kiss Zambia with genuine passion. But I'll tell you, I'm right there, and I believe there is genuine passion. It's a disaster."

I exhaled. "You know what? That sounds stressful. But the play isn't until tomorrow, so why don't you relax for tonight? Come back to the farmhouse. Miss May and I will make you your favorite cookies."

Germany nodded. "Perhaps that would be nice. A plate of cookies could be just what the doctor ordered."

I smiled. "Great."

Germany squeezed my hand. I could tell he felt a little better, and that made me proud. It was early in our relationship so I was still trying to earn good girlfriend points.

Germany and I were headed toward the exit when Master Skinner stormed into the restaurant. Master Skinner was a sensei who owned the local dojo in town. He was also a cast member in Germany's play. An understudy for the lead, Adam.

Germany took a step back when Skinner entered. Skinner pointed right at Germany. "You. I knew you would be here, dining out in an upscale casual setting while the production is in shambles. We need to talk."

Germany held up both his hands in surrender. "I'd be happy to talk tomorrow, Master Skinner. But right now I'm headed home."

Master Skinner balled up one of his famous fists of fury.

"On second thought," said Germany. "What would you like to discuss?"

"I want the part," said Skinner. "I was not meant to be an understudy. Adam is a hack. I doubt he was ever on Broadway."

"I've seen the playbills," said Germany.

"You can fake that stuff," Skinner said. "Easy. Photoshop. Point is, Adam doesn't have the talent to back up his claims."

I stepped forward. "Miss May saw him in a performance of CATS. Back in the 80s, I think. Supposedly he was a very good cat."

Skinner shook his head. "You don't need talent to be a

cat. Purr, purr." Skinner licked an imaginary paw. "That's not acting. It's child's play. Now give me that lead role for tomorrow's performance, Germany. Give me the role or you will regret it."

Germany's face reddened. "You shouldn't threaten me like that. I am your director."

"I'm not threatening you. I'm just promising you, Adam will botch this performance. I feel it in my bones, and my bones are never wrong, Germany. Never!" Skinner was rarely this worked up, and I could tell it rattled Germany.

I put my hand on Germany's arm. "It's OK, Germany. Let's just go home."

Germany glared at Master Skinner. I had never seen Germany so upset. Honestly, I didn't hate it. The fire in his eyes made his bowtie less "cute boy" and more "James Bond at a casino."

"You're right, Chelsea. I can't worry about this. If Master Skinner doesn't want to be an understudy, then he need not show up at the play tomorrow."

Skinner tossed his head back and laughed. "Oh, good one, Germany. You'll see. Just wait." With that, Skinner stormed back outside into the rainy night.

Germany sighed. I felt bad for him, having to deal with so many complicated personalities.

He might even need more than cookies to help soothe this tension.

## 2

## ACTING OUT

*T*he morning after I had dinner with Germany, I met Miss May and Teeny for breakfast at my number one favorite restaurant in Pine Grove, *Grandma's*. *Grandma's* belonged to Teeny's mom, Granny, but Teeny was the brains and brawn behind the operation. The place was cute as could be. Brick exterior with a charming green awning out front. And no matter the time of day, it was packed with the people of Pine Grove, chatting and enjoying one of Teeny's home-cooked delicacies.

I approached, walking my puppy, Steve, and stopped a few feet outside the entrance. I knelt down and looked the dog in the eyes. "Steve," I said. "Listen. You'll have to sit outside while I eat breakfast, OK?"

Steve whimpered.

"I know," I said. "It's not fun being leashed outside the restaurant. But I don't want to get Teeny in trouble. And if she lets me bring you inside, she has to let her other regulars bring their dogs, and it's a whole big thing. You understand, right?"

Steve cocked his head and plopped down on the sidewalk. Even though he was still technically a puppy, and he walked with the same cute limp he'd always had, Steve had gotten much bigger since Germany had given the dog to me several months ago.

Steve had the personality of an adorable toddler and the body of a grown dog. Imagine if Stone Cold Steve Austin walked and talked like Shirley Temple — that was my puppy. I tied Steve up to a bike rack and went inside.

I entered to find almost every seat in the restaurant taken. The energetic buzz of conversation filled the air. Waiters bustled in every direction. But Teeny didn't worry about working too hard. She sat in the back of the restaurant, at our favorite booth, chatting with Miss May.

I smiled when I saw them. Miss May and Teeny made a cute pair. Teeny was, well, very tiny. She had a puff of blonde hair and a smile that might as well have been a neon sign. Miss May, my aunt and adoptive parent, was big and broad and moved thoughtfully. That morning, my aunt wore her trademark blue jeans with a flannel, glasses perched on the end of her nose.

Teeny squealed when she saw me. "Chelsea. You're finally here. Where have you been? It doesn't matter. Tell us about the fight."

"What fight?"

Miss May crossed her arms. "You know what fight. The scuffle between your boyfriend and Master Skinner. Everyone is talking about it."

I slid into the booth. It surprised me I had already forgotten about the tense moment between Germany and Master Skinner. And I definitely should have realized that the townspeople would blow the brief confrontation way out of proportion.

"It wasn't a scuffle," I said.

Teeny poured me a cup of coffee, then added almost equal parts sugar. "That's not what we heard. We heard you physically restrained Germany. And Master Skinner balled up his fists of fury and growled like an angry dog."

I chuckled. "No one growled."

Teeny and Miss May leaned forward in unison, like synchronized swimmers.

I sighed. "You two will not let me have breakfast until I tell you this story, will you?"

Teeny raised her eyebrows. "The kitchen is closed to Chelsea until Chelsea spills the proverbial refried beans."

"How would you spill refried beans?" I asked. "Wouldn't they kind of slide out of the can?"

"I make my refried beans from scratch, Chelsea," said Teeny. "And trust me. I've spilled them. Not fun to clean up."

Miss May cringed. "Gross. Refried beans everywhere. What do you do for that?"

Teeny shrugged. "Start with paper towels, that gets up most of it. Then get a waiter to scrub for as long as it takes to de-bean."

Miss May chuckled. "I forgot you have waiters to do the dirty work."

"Oh, I do not. I just know how to delegate. Can we focus on the drama from last night?" Teeny said. "I'm sure Chelsea's hungry so we should let her tell the story."

Teeny was right. I was hungry. So I obliged. Told the story with as many details as I could remember. Miss May and Teeny thrived on gossip. They gobbled up every word like it was a freshly baked treat. And I'll admit, it was satisfying retelling the tale.

When I concluded the story, Teeny placed her palms on the table and stood up. "OK. Great job, Chelsea. You have earned one of my world-famous tarts."

Miss May looked up at Teeny. "You make tarts?"

Teeny nodded. "Starting today I do. And they're already world famous."

Teeny hurried away. Miss May and I laughed.

"I bet these tarts are good," I said.

Miss May nodded. "Everything Teeny makes is good."

A few minutes later, Teeny set three perfect tarts on the table. They were big. At least four inches in diameter. Fresh raspberry compote oozed over the edges. The tart was dusted with powdered sugar and looked like an image cut straight from a magazine. Or printed from the Internet or something. Do they even make magazines anymore? Not important. The tarts looked good.

"Teeny," said Miss May. "You've outdone yourself."

Teeny smiled. "I know."

"But you serve these for breakfast?" Miss May asked. "It looks like a dessert."

Teeny dismissed Miss May with a wave of the hand. "Breakfast and dessert are the same thing, just on opposite sides of night. Taste it."

Miss May and I reached out and each took a tart. The thing was so delicate I handled it like it was a live stick of dynamite. Until, of course, I took a big, sloppy bite. The raspberry was tart, tangy, and sweet. Real chunks of raspberry melded together with a gooey, thick, homemade syrup. And the cookie crust was flaky, buttery, delicious shortbread. *Mmmm. Did I mention buttery?*

Teeny leaned forward. "How is it?"

Miss May wiped her mouth. "Can't you tell by the way we're eating in total silence? These things are incredible."

I nodded. "World-famous."

Teeny cackled and smacked the table with glee. "I knew

it. I knew they were world famous. Oh boy, I'm glad you like them. Are you two just saying that?"

I responded with my mouth full. "Nope. These are delicious."

Teeny smirked and smacked the table again. Miss May and I laughed. Spending time together at Teeny's restaurant always felt good, especially when Teeny had a new delicacy to share. Although, the delicacies didn't matter, not really. All that mattered was time with family and friends. Sure, being a guinea pig for amazing food was a perk, but it wasn't the point.

I had spent so many years living away from home, for school, for work, for my relationship... I had always known that I was missing out on big events, like birthdays and holidays. But I hadn't realized all the small moments I had missed, like sitting at Teeny's restaurant, laughing on a random Friday morning. I felt a surge of joy, of gratitude, just to be in a familiar booth in a familiar place with people I loved completely.

Until, of course... The moment was interrupted.

Someone pushed the front door of the restaurant open with a bang and charged toward our table. His high, nasal voice gave me a pretty good idea of who it was. "Chelsea. Teeny. Miss May. I hear you three have been gossiping about the community production of *Phantom of the Opera*."

I turned. Sure enough, there was Adam Smith. The notorious lead actor from the community theater. He was wearing black slacks and a turtleneck. And his hair had been slicked back behind his ears. Classic actor.

"Is that true, ladies? Have you been spreading rumors of infighting among the cast and crew?"

I wrinkled my nose. "I'm confused. You're angry because

we're talking about how everyone in the play has been fighting?"

"All that matters is the work. People always lose sight of that. Don't you worry about our process. We are dramatists. Our passion infuses our work. It's not meant to be discussed by the people in town. We are performers. We are meant to remain pure. We are not meant to be ground up in the local rumor mill like common oats."

Teeny chuckled. "Adam. You really are dramatic. A little gossip never hurt anyone. Besides, Chelsea was there. Your understudy verbally attacked her boyfriend. I heard he growled."

"No one growled," I said. "And I'm sorry for gossiping, Adam. You're right. We should support local theater, not grind it up in the rumor mill. I'm sure the show will be very good."

The town lawyer, Tom Gigley, popped his white-haired head up from the booth behind us. "Hey, I don't care if you actors hate each other. Live theater is such a thrill. I hope you get into an argument on stage. Maybe a fistfight breaks out. Then I'll get my money's worth."

Teeny pointed at Tom to show her agreement. "Well said, Tom. The more these people hate each other, the less boring the play will be. I bet these rumors are helping ticket sales."

I shook my head. "The play will not be boring, even if no one gets into a fistfight. Germany has worked hard on this production."

Adam crossed his arms. "We have all worked hard on this production. We have poured our souls into it. Committed our lives to theater and the dramatic arts. Please respect that." Adam waved his arm wide, gesturing at the people dining in the restaurant. "All of you. Respect our privacy. Support our art. That is all we ask."

Adam turned and hightailed it out of the restaurant with his nose pointed skyward.

Miss May chuckled. "If Adam is the lead in the play, I'm sure it will be very exciting."

If only Miss May knew how right she would be... Pine Grove's production of *Phantom* was about to have more thrills than all of Broadway combined.

## 3

## DEAD MAN TALKING

The Pine Grove community theater sat right in the center of town, near the gazebo and the walking track. The theater was in a two-story brick building with a big parking lot. There was a playground off to the side for bored children. And when there was no play going on, the stage was often home to dance classes, knitting clubs, or preschool groups on field trips.

On opening night, there was an electric hum in the air. Dozens of audience members gathered out front, excited for the town production of *Phantom of the Opera*.

An elderly lady with big, gray hair pushed and shoved her way toward will-call. Girl Scouts sold cookies out front. Humphrey, a *Grandma's* regular and curmudgeon-about-town, went from person to person with a bucket, selling raffle tickets to benefit the town's next production.

Miss May smiled and nudged me with her elbow as we approached. "Don't you love live theater?"

I nodded. "I loved it way more before Germany got involved. This stuff is stressful."

Miss May shook her head. "It's a good stress. The stress

that comes from working with people. Building something together. Creating an experience that will delight your friends and neighbors and will be talked about for years to come."

"You two wait up." Teeny rushed toward us from the parking lot. "I thought we were meeting at my restaurant. What happened?"

Miss May crinkled her eyes. "We never said we were meeting at your restaurant."

Teeny's eyes widened. "Then who was I supposed to meet at the restaurant?" Teeny crossed her arms. "And why were they late?"

Miss May shrugged. "I'm not sure. But if you want candy, we better get inside."

"I want a lot of candy," said Teeny. "I bet Chelsea does too."

I smiled. "You know me so well."

Excited audience members crowded the lobby of the theater. There was a line for the women's room that snaked out toward the front door. But there was no line for the men's room. That was always how it worked.

A bored teenage girl sold candy behind a folding table. Teeny approached with a big smile. "Hey there. I'll take one of everything."

The teenage girl cocked her head. "You want one of every candy?" She spoke in a drawling monotone that almost made me laugh.

I stepped forward. "Teeny loves candy. I bet she'll come back for more at intermission."

"If everything goes according to plan, I'm going to sneak out during the first act and reload," said Teeny. I wasn't sure if Teeny was serious or not, but the lady loved her sweets.

The girl shrugged and rang Teeny up. Teeny leaned in

with a conspiratorial whisper. "Have you heard about all the fighting in the cast? Do you think there will be fireworks tonight?"

The teenage girl shrugged. "I'm just doing community service hours for my church group. I don't pay attention to the gossip. But if I paid attention to the gossip, I'd expect a wild fist fight. Every actor in this play hates each other. And I hear they hate the weird director even more."

"Hey," I said. "That weird director is my boyfriend."

The teen girl looked down. "Sorry I called him weird."

I shrugged. "It's OK. He is weird. It's his best quality."

The lights in the lobby flickered. Miss May rubbed her hands together. Her eyes sparkled. "Better go get our seats, ladies. It's going to start in a couple minutes."

"I think we might have some time," Teeny said. "Looks like they're experiencing some difficulties with the lights."

"The lights aren't flickering because they're having difficulties," I said. "Flickering lights are the international symbol for the start of a play."

"I know, Chelsea. I'm joking," Teeny said. "Gosh, sometimes it's so easy to make you think I'm some kind of dumb blonde. I'm not! I've been to dozens of shows down in the city."

"Hey, I'm blonde too," I said. "I don't make any assumptions based on hair color."

The lights flickered again. Miss May walked toward the theater. "Let's get our seats."

If you've never seen a small-town production of the *Phantom of the Opera*, I can't recommend it highly enough. *Phantom* is a challenging play, to say the least. The parts require excellent singers, phenomenal actors, and world-class set design. Most small towns don't have access to those things and the creative workarounds are entertaining. OK, at least our town didn't have access to those things. Not so sure about yours.

So Germany had taken some, um...creative liberties to accommodate for the lack of budget and resources.

The sets for Pine Grove's production of *Phantom* were mostly made of cardboard. The costumes had been borrowed from another small-town production and they did not fit the actors well. Our local actors struggled to hit the high notes.

Still, the play was entertaining. Possibly more entertaining than the Broadway production, because of how much I enjoyed seeing familiar faces on stage.

Brian, the owner of the coffee shop in town, had several lines. He delivered them all perfectly. I clapped extra hard after his scene.

Adam Smith, however, the lead in the play? He had worse luck remembering his lines. His performance was awkward and clunky. I wondered if Germany had been correct to deny Master Skinner the lead role. Skinner at least had charisma. Adam was odd and awkward.

About halfway through the second act, there was a scene where Adam and the female lead, Zambia, had a romantic meal together. My eyes widened as they took stage together. I nudged Miss May. "I think this is the kiss. Coming up."

Miss May nudged Teeny and whispered the same thing. Teeny nudged whoever was next to her. The whole theater played a hushed game of telephone, waiting for the kiss.

Adam and Zambia looked out at the audience, sensing the excited frenzy. Then Adam stood and took Zambia's hands in his. Zambia stepped toward him. Adam wrapped his arm around her waist. She leaned forward. They kissed.

The first five seconds of the kiss seemed normal. But the lip lock did not stop after five seconds. It did not stop after ten seconds. It did not stop after fifteen seconds. Twenty seconds into the kiss and people were hooting and hollering from the crowd. I looked over at Miss May and Teeny. They were cracking up with laughter. I looked back at Adam and Zambia in disbelief... The kiss was still going! Finally, the two separated. Adam wiped his lips. The audience erupted with laughter.

An angry woman pushed her way out from the center of a row then stormed up the aisle, toward the exit. My eyes widened. "Is that...?"

Miss May nodded. "That's Dorothy. Adam's wife."

Teeny covered her eyes. "I can't look. Tell me when she's gone."

The door slammed. "OK. She's gone," I said.

Up on stage, the scene concluded. After another minute, Adam and Zambia exited stage left. The rest of the play continued without much drama.

That is, until the end.

Adam took center stage for the last scene of the play. He delivered a concluding monologue, pacing the stage. His character was upset for some reason or another, I don't remember why.

"Life is long," Adam announced. "For some of us, it's short. The sky is blue. But for some of us, it's green."

Teeny nudged me. "What is he talking about?"

I shrugged and pointed back at the stage. Adam opened a box of pastries and held a tart to his chest.

"This tart is a symbol of my love. I shall break it in half. I shall keep part of this tart with me at all times to remember my love. She will stay with me always. And she will––"

Bang. Bang. The sound of a gunshot echoed in the theater. Adam doubled over, then fell backwards. He reached up to the sky and delivered his final line. "My tart. My heart."

There was a moment of quiet in the theater. Then applause rippled across the room. Seconds later, and everyone in the theater was on their feet for a standing ovation. Miss May, Teeny, and I joined the crowd. Yes, much of the play had been confusing and weird. But the finale had had a resounding impact. Cheers boomed throughout the theater. I saw an old woman wipe a tear from the corner of her eye.

After a few seconds of the standing ovation, Zambia rushed out onto the stage, no longer wearing her costume. She knelt down beside Adam and screamed. "That wasn't part of the play! He's been shot. Adam has been shot."

Germany rushed out beside Zambia. He pumped on Adam's chest. Listened for a heartbeat.

Appreciation and applause morphed into unsettled shrieks and panicked conversation.

It seemed Adam Smith, not his character, had been shot. Audience members rushed for the exit but Miss May, Teeny, and I stayed in our seats, necks craned, looking toward the stage.

Police rushed toward the theater stage as audience members rushed toward the exits. I couldn't look away from the stage. Blood covered Germany's hands. Zambia continued crying, rocking back and forth in stunned grief.

Someone murdered Adam Smith. And it would be up to me, Miss May, and Teeny to find the killer and bring justice to our small town, once again.

4

## ADAM BOMB

*a* dam Smith was not the first person who had been murdered in Pine Grove. *You probably know that already*. Our little town had been unlucky in the last year and we had seen quite a few murder victims. Miss May and I had investigated each of those murders. With Teeny, we'd found the killers and restored peace to Pine Grove.

*What I'm trying to say is...*

Adam Smith was the first person whose murder I'd actually witnessed. Every time Miss May and I had investigated a case prior to that night at the theater, we'd stumbled onto the crime scene after the act. Let me tell you, it's never good when someone dies... but when someone dies right in front of you, it's really bad.

I wondered, how could anyone end a life like that? I hated the reminder, so up close and personal, that there was evil in this world. And that even the most charming small towns could not be guarded from treachery. I thought of the audience in the theater when John Wilkes Booth had assassinated Lincoln. Sure, this was all happening on a smaller scale, but it still felt chilling and dramatic.

It's not like bad things hadn't happened in Pine Grove before. Our little town had experienced more than its fair share of bad news recently. But this was different. This was happening right before my eyes. I didn't move for at least two minutes as people streamed out of the theater and the police rushed toward the stage. Miss May and Teeny didn't move either.

Perhaps their minds were racing with theories and suspicions... Questions we would need to answer to solve the mystery. Not me. I'm not sure I had a single thought beyond, "Wow. I'm scared."

I snapped back to reality as Miss May took a firm hold of my wrist. "Chelsea. Are you OK?"

I slowly turned my head toward Miss May.

"I've been saying your name. No answer," she said. "You're in shock."

I pointed toward the stage. "Adam... He was shot."

Miss May swallowed. "I know."

Teeny leaned forward and looked in my eyes. "We will find the person who did this, right?"

I stammered. Miss May nodded. "Absolutely. This shooting isn't just a crime that was perpetrated on Adam. He was killed in front of everyone. We all had to witness this atrocity. The shooting was a crime perpetrated against everyone in this room."

I nodded. "Everyone in this town."

Miss May set her mouth, hard and determined. "You're right. This was a crime against Pine Grove. We have no choice but to solve it."

Teeny balled up one of her tiny little hands. "Let's get to it, then. Let's find the bad guy."

Suddenly, I had a panicked realization. "Germany! Germany must be so upset."

We found Germany pacing in front of the stage near the orchestra pit, wringing his hands. His eyes widened when he saw me. "Chelsea. Chelsea!"

Germany wrapped me up in a hug. I hugged him back. Miss May and Teeny stood a few feet away, holding hands. "Thank God the three of you are here," said Germany. "Poor Adam. What a terrible thing. He deserves justice, swift and cold, as you always serve it."

Miss May stepped forward. "I agree. Let's begin the investigation now. We all know there was some conflict within this theater troupe. Can you tell us anything more that might be helpful?"

Germany cast a look toward the stage. The police had cordoned off the area around Adam with caution tape. Analysts crouched beside the body. Chief Sunshine Flanagan and Detective Wayne Hudson took careful notes and spoke in hushed whispers.

Germany turned back to us. "Are you sure we should talk about this here?"

Miss May looked past Germany, at the cops on stage. "They're busy. Documenting the wrong details, I'm sure. Foolishly neglecting to interview you."

"Has anyone talked to you?" I asked.

Germany shook his head. "No. They told me to wait over here. Asked me to get out of the way. Quite rude. I'm the director of this play. I know these people better than their own parents. I know their fears and their insecurities and what makes them tick."

Teeny bit her lip. "Great. If you know all that, maybe you know who killed Adam."

Germany exhaled. "I wish. Alas, I don't have a clue."

Teeny threw up her hands. "I thought you knew these

people so well. Their inside souls and their deepest secrets or whatever."

"I was speaking artistically. In the artistic sense they have exposed me to their most vulnerable selves. In practice, my actors rarely opened up to me. I'm sorry. I was talking out of my behind, as they say. Don't judge me. My lead actor was shot and killed and I'm not thinking straight."

I took Germany's hand. "We would never judge you." I looked over at Teeny and Miss May. "Right?"

Teeny and Miss May mumbled something about how they didn't judge Germany. It wasn't convincing.

"Turtle." Wayne called out to Germany from up on stage. "Get up here. We need to talk."

Wayne's gruff tone rankled me. "Hey," I said. "Please be polite, Detective."

Wayne shrugged. "All I said is that we need to talk."

"Your tone was very rude," I said.

Germany put his hand on my arm. "It's fine, Chelsea. I'd be happy to speak with Detective Hudson. And his tone did not offend me."

Germany approached the edge of the stage and tried to hoist himself up. He flopped onto his stomach, got onto his hands and knees, and slowly stood. Wayne rolled his eyes as he watched Germany fumble. Sometimes that Turtle moved a lot like his namesake. Awkward, slow, graceless, but somehow still cute.

Teeny nudged me as she watched Germany stand and speak to Wayne. "Looks like we've got two pointy edges of an isosceles love triangle on our hands."

I shook my head. "No. I told Wayne around Christmas. He and I will not be an item. I'm with Germany now."

Wayne looked over at me from up on stage. It was a

glance that maybe, I could possibly admit, had a tinge of longing.

Teeny smirked. "Not so sure Wayne got the message."

"Yeah, yeah. Everyone loves Chelsea. Very dramatic. Very romantic. But can we talk about this case?" Miss May licked her lips. "Flanagan is so preoccupied she hasn't kicked us out of the theater yet. Let's try to gather some clues."

I nodded. "Good idea. But how are we going to gather clues from down here? The dead body's on the stage."

"This crime isn't like the others we've investigated," said Miss May. "The killer was nowhere near the victim."

I nodded. "True. The shooter could have been anywhere in this room."

"So this entire theater is the scene of the crime," said Teeny.

Miss May touched her nose. "Exactly."

Miss May turned and looked up at the mezzanine. "I suspect the shooter was sitting somewhere up there. Or in one of the boxes off to the side."

"Like those grumpy old men in the *Muppets*," said Teeny. "Those guys always seemed like shooters to me."

"So let's try to go up there," I said. My eyes widened. "Oh my goodness. Maybe we shouldn't. How do we know the killer has even left the building?"

Teeny gave me a dismissive wave. "You know karate. We'll be fine."

I furrowed my brow. "Karate is not effective against bullets."

Teeny shrugged. "That's never stopped you before."

"Hey." Deputy Hercules pointed at us from up on stage. "What are the three of you doing in here?"

Police Chief Sunshine Flanagan followed Hercules' gaze.

With her stunning eyes and shiny red hair, Flanagan seemed more like a TV cop than a real-life cop. But there she was. Glaring right at me with her arms crossed. "How did I forget the Three Stooges? Escort them out, Hercules. Make an arrest if you have to."

Miss May held up her hands. "We don't need an arrest. Or an escort. We're going."

Flanagan pointed to the exit. "Good. Go. Now."

Miss May turned and trudged up the aisle, toward the exit. Teeny and I followed. As we walked, images from the play flashed through my head. I remembered Dorothy, Adam's wife, charging up the same aisle. I remembered Zambia sharing a long and passionate kiss with Adam. And I remembered the anger in Master Skinner's eyes the prior night. I also remembered Germany's distant, distressed attitude.

I wrapped my arms around myself as I walked.

Adam Smith had been assassinated.

And so many people had wanted him dead... Including my boyfriend.

## 5

## WHAT'S THE SCOOP

*A*fter Hercules kicked us out of the theater, Miss May, Teeny, and I headed over to *Grandma's* to debrief. By the time we got to the restaurant, there was a line out the door and onto the sidewalk.

We slowed as we approached from the parking lot. Every audience member from the play seemed to have had the same idea we did. And they had all called their friends to come gossip. It was a sea of grave but curious faces. Like a convention of morbid rubberneckers.

A mother bounced a toddler in her arms as she spoke with her husband. A teenage girl texted furiously with a wrinkled brow. The local reporter, Liz, moved from person to person, getting quotes about what had happened at the play.

Teeny shook her head as we approached. "My goodness. Why does tragedy always have to be good for the comfort food business?"

I shrugged. "Communities gather when bad things happen. Your restaurant is so cozy. It makes sense."

Liz approached, holding out a small recording device.

"The world's most famous amateur detectives. I was hoping you would show. What did you learn at the scene of the crime?"

Miss May reached out and gently lowered the recording device. "Please turn that off, Liz. We learned nothing."

Liz turned off the recording device. "Even if you did, you wouldn't tell me."

"But we always give you the story when it's ready, right?" Miss May arched her eyebrows.

Liz hovered her finger above the record button on her device. "Then don't give me a quote as an amateur detective. Give me a quote as an audience member who was at the play. What did you think when the shot rang out?"

"I'm sorry, Liz. You know we can't give a scoop like that," said May.

"I'd be happy to give you a scoop of fresh, hot soup, though," said Teeny. "We've got vegetable barley tonight."

Liz grumbled. "Maybe later. Thanks."

We entered the restaurant and a waitress rushed by with three dishes balanced on her arm. Another waitress crossed in the opposite direction. The restaurant was loud and chaotic. The staff clearly needed help.

Teeny looked around and put her head in her hand. "This is nuts."

"It's OK," said Miss May. "Why don't Chelsea and I pitch in? It looks like you're short a couple servers. Chelsea, you take the front room. I'll bus tables."

Teeny's eyes widened. "Really? You'll help?"

Miss May give Teeny a nice smile. "We've been eating free at your restaurant for decades. It's the least we can do."

The restaurant remained busy until closing at 11 PM. By then, my feet hurt and I was sweaty. Which, to be fair, was a pretty normal condition for me. Either way, I felt proud to have helped Teeny.

When the final guest left, Teeny locked the door then turned to me and Miss May. "Group hug," Teeny said, and wrapped us both in her small but firm arms. "Thank you both, so much. I couldn't have done this without you."

"Please," Miss May said, "you would have been fine."

Teeny shoved us toward our booth in the back. "Sit down. We're all having a big bowl of soup. We need to talk about this case."

The soup was delicious. It was thick and hearty, with big chunks of celery and carrots. The barley was perfectly chewy and moist. It sank to the bottom like buried treasure. Every bite made me feel nourished and warm.

"This is why your restaurant gets so crowded when things get bad in Pine Grove," I said. "You're an incredible cook, Teeny. And this is true comfort food. Like putting a pair of sweatpants on my tongue."

"And the two of you are incredible sleuths," said Teeny, deferring the compliment as she was wont to do. "So let's talk suspects."

"The first one is obvious." Miss May slurped a spoonful of soup. "Chelsea, would you like to do the honors?"

I groaned. "I'd rather not. It's depressing."

Teeny leaned forward. "What? What's depressing? You gotta tell me now."

"Who was in charge of the production?" I said. "Who was seen arguing with the victim? Who did the victim openly hate?"

Teeny gasped and covered her mouth. "Germany Turtle. Germany Turtle is a suspect!?"

I didn't like talking about this, but I knew it was true. "I'm sure he will be. The cops are going to talk to him carefully," I said. "Plus, I have a hunch that Wayne will be extra hard on Germany. And Germany says so much stupid stuff. His mouth is always going. He might incriminate himself without knowing it."

Teeny shook her head. "That poor sweet kid. Sometimes smart people seem so stupid."

Miss May chuckled. "Germany is the best example of that in the history of time. He's done award-winning lion research, but he puts his foot in his mouth more than Chelsea does."

"Hey," I said. "OK. That's fair. I'm smart but I seem stupid, too."

Miss May laughed. "It's not a competition."

"But Germany is not the only suspect," said Teeny. "Everyone hated Adam. And he publicly cheated on his wife less than an hour before he got shot."

Miss May shrugged. "I'm not sure I would call that cheating."

"I would," I said. "I read the script. Nowhere in that document did it specify that Adam's character should have kissed Zambia's character for an entire minute. With tongue. In front of the entire town."

Teeny giggled. "Chelsea."

"I'm just saying. That was not necessary. It was gratuitous."

Teeny looked over at Miss May with a smirk. "Now Chelsea is using big words to prove she's smart."

"Whatever," I said. "Dorothy is definitely a suspect. Maybe she never left the theater tonight. Perhaps she went upstairs and got revenge."

"Dark but plausible." Miss May salted her soup.

"It doesn't need salt, May." Teeny shook her head. "I

salted it to perfection. I also peppered it to perfection. The soup was seasoned to perfection."

"I agree," I said.

Miss May took a bite of soup, making a point to ignore us. "Master Skinner is another obvious suspect. He felt he deserved the part. He hated Adam."

"More than that," I said. "If Adam is dead... When the lead actor dies... Doesn't the understudy get the role?"

"I suppose. But I doubt Master Skinner would have assumed that there would be another performance after the lead character was murdered on stage."

"Not so sure about that," said Teeny. "What's that old expression? 'The show must flow gong?'"

"The show must go on," I said.

"That's definitely not it," said Teeny. "Look at you, trying to seem smart again."

"The expression is definitely the show must go on," I said.

"Dorothy and Skinner are both good suspects," said Miss May. "But before we go down either of those proverbial rabbit holes, I think we need to take a closer look at the scene of the crime."

"That place is swarming with cops," I said.

Miss May shrugged. "So we'll give it a couple of hours. Head over there around 2 AM."

My eyes bugged. "Tonight?"

"That's too late for me," Teeny said. "I gotta open *Grandma's* bright and early."

"Yeah," I said. "Maybe we should just, sleep on this whole situation?"

Miss May shook her head. "Let's not forget, Chelsea... There's an assassin on the loose in Pine Grove."

## 6

## THE SHOW MUST FLOW GONG

*I*'ve never liked napping. I'm not a morning person, and waking up from a nap feels like waking up way too early in the morning, no matter what time of day it actually is.

But Miss May has always been a big believer in naps. So we headed back to the farmhouse after the soup at Teeny's so Miss May could power nap.

While Miss May slept, I tried to keep my mind occupied in all sorts of ways. First, I fed Steve, who ate his food in about seven seconds flat. He looked up at me, like, "More?" I gave him a treat, then played fetch with him for what felt like a half an hour but was actually about two and a half minutes.

Then I cleaned the farmhouse kitchen so it was spick and span. Steve followed close on my heels the whole time, waiting for crumbs to drop. He was always a helpful cleaning partner. Who needs a vacuum when you have a giant, hungry puppy?

Then, for some reason, I decided to bake a big batch of dark chocolate, macadamia cookies. Once the cookies were ready, I ate six. That made me feel a little shaky and queasy for about twenty minutes. Once the sugar shakes subsided, I cleaned up the mess I made while baking. I looked at the clock. It was 12:30 AM. Miss May didn't want to head out until 1 or 2 AM. *Ugh.*

I grabbed Steve's leash, pulled on my favorite old sweatshirt, and headed outside. Steve immediately peed on the muddy lawn, then seemed eager to head back inside. He didn't like getting the cold March sludge all over his big paws.

But I had another destination in mind. I turned and trudged down toward the barn to chat with my favorite confidant, See-Saw. See-Saw was the farm's resident tiny horse. With her mottled coat and soft mane, See-Saw was a fan favorite among visitors to the orchard. But she was also a great listener, as long as I provided food to keep her occupied. And she never hesitated to share her honest opinion in the form of grunting, stamping, or taking a poop.

I entered the barn carrying a basket of carrots. Steve immediately started sniffing around, fascinated by the strange odors of the barn.

Luckily for me, See-Saw was awake. She gave me a little snort when I stepped inside then waddled over toward me and ate a carrot straight out of the basket. *Did I mention See-Saw was a spoiled little horse?* KP, Miss May's farmhand, was See-Saw's caretaker, and he tended to overindulge her.

As See-Saw ate, I explained every detail of what had happened that night. A few times, I interrupted myself to scold Steve, usually something like, "Don't eat that!" Unfortunately, Steve wanted to eat most things in the barn so the interruptions were more frequent than I would have liked. See-Saw seemed irritated by Steve's immaturity, but the wise old horse listened intently, nonetheless.

See-Saw looked over at me with compassion as I told her how much I was worried about Germany. Her eyes widened as I told her how Zambia stormed the stage, screaming and crying. And See-Saw let out an angry snort when I told her how rude Wayne had been to Germany.

After twenty minutes of talking, I began to feel like I was the one being rude, prattling on about my problems to a captive audience. I was about to ask See-Saw how she had been doing when my phone rang. It was Germany. Just in case I hadn't heard the phone, Steve started barking to let me know there was a new sound.

"Thanks, Steve," I said. "I got it." I answered the phone. "Hey," I said to Germany. "Can't sleep?"

Germany responded in a sad monotone. "I haven't even tried to sleep. My mind is racing. I keep hearing the bang of the gun. Seeing Adam fall. It's terrible. Not at all what we rehearsed."

I sat on a little stool beside See-Saw and gave her a pat on the back. "I know. You had spent so much time with Adam, you must feel awful."

"Awful is an understatement. There is no word for how I feel. Devastated? Heart-wrenched? Shattered to my very core?"

Even in grief, Germany had a flair for the dramatic.

"You should try to sleep though, really," I said as I fed See-Saw another carrot. "It's important to stay rested and healthy during stressful times, otherwise everything gets worse. Maybe eat some vegetables and get in bed."

"I can't eat vegetables at a time like this," said Germany. "If it's not creamy or fried, don't come knocking."

Steve barked softly, like, "I hear that."

I ran my hand along See-Saw's beautiful coat. "OK. If you insist."

"I'm sorry for calling so late," Germany said. "Were you sleeping?"

"No, no. I'm with See-Saw. It's fine."

"I thought I heard the sound of horse chewing."

I laughed. "She doesn't have the best table manners. Chews with her mouth open all the time." See-Saw glared at me. I chuckled. "What? It's true. Steve is here too, wanna say hi?" I held out the phone and Steve let out a cute little yip. I put the phone back to my ear.

Germany cleared his throat, still serious. "I'm actually calling because I have something I need to ask you...about the play."

I gulped. My mind raced with possibilities. Had Germany witnessed something related to the murder? Did someone threaten him? My body stiffened. See-Saw's body tensed, and Steve growled from across the barn.

"Of course," I said. "Anything. What do you need to ask me?"

"I'm thinking... I want to honor Adam. And the best way to honor him is if we continue with the production."

I cocked my head, unsure if I had heard Germany right. "You want to put on the play again tomorrow night?"

"That's right."

"Germany. That's a...strange idea. The shooter hasn't been found. The theater is probably still an active crime scene. Continuing with the production could be dangerous. Especially since someone in the cast or crew could be a killer! It's so stupid. How can you be so smart and so stupid at the same time?"

Germany replied with confidence and poise. "I love this small town. It's a town with strength, character, and grit. No matter how many people are murdered here, the denizens persevere. Not a single person has moved away since the first victim was found over a year ago. I want to embody that dogged spirit in the production of this play. I'm still relatively new here and it's important that I demonstrate that I'm just as strong as this town. I want to show everyone here that they inspire me, and in turn I'd like to inspire them."

I shook my head. My cheeks reddened. "That's ridiculous, Germany."

Germany seemed unshaken by my doubt. "I'm afraid you cannot talk me out of this."

"Then why did you call me?" I asked.

Germany stammered, unsure of his reply for the first time. "I don't know. I guess I expected you to be blindly supportive."

"Right," I said. "I should go. I'm being rude to See-Saw."

I hung up before Germany had a chance to reply. "That is so ridiculous." See-Saw stomped her back foot. I could tell she agreed.

There was a soft knock on the barn door door behind me. Steve barked, an excited, happy bark, so I knew it wasn't a scary intruder. I turned. There was Miss May, dressed to go out. "Everything OK?"

"Everything's fine. Germany's an idiot."

Miss May nodded. I could tell by the look on her face... She had heard a lot of the conversation. "Ready to go?"

I nodded. And we headed back to the scene of the crime.

## 7

## AND, SCENE!

*T*he town theater had a creepy energy after dark. Or maybe the creepy energy was because of how recently the stage had been the scene of a murder. Either way, I had an uneasy feeling tingling in my fingers and toes as we approached. Miss May walked with such confident strides. But I took baby steps, like I was about to enter a freezing cold pool.

"Are you sure we should do this?" I asked.

"I'm sure."

"Maybe we should come back with Teeny in the morning. Or maybe we should go over to her house now to make sure she doesn't want to come."

"Teeny needs her sleep. She said so herself, she has to open up the restaurant early. It might be the off-season for us up at the orchard but her kitchen never has an off-day. Besides, we can't come here during business hours. The police will be back."

I stopped and looked at the theater. "OK. But how are we going to get inside? We can't break into the theater. I'm almost positive I saw a security system. It's not worth the risk."

"Chelsea. Stop doing your scaredy-cat routine. You know this is part of the sleuthing gig. Sneaking in places doesn't usually bother you so much"

"First of all," I said, "yes it does. I'm always trying to talk us out of going into spooky, dark places. Second of all, this is different. We saw a man get shot right in front of us today. Inside this building."

Miss May walked around the theater. There was a small door on the side of the building marked "actors entrance." She walked right up to the door and knocked three times.

I stayed a few feet back. "What are you doing?"

Miss May turned back and smirked at me. "I have a plan, as always. I wanted to surprise you."

The door opened with a loud creak. There stood Petunia, an elderly woman famous in town for her prowess at the poker tables. Petunia was rough around the edges. And rough in the middle. Rough all around. But she had been helpful on previous cases so I felt a weird sense of relief when I saw her. Even though she was one of the meanest old ladies I'd ever met.

"Miss May and little single Chelsea," Petunia growled. "So we meet again."

"How do you know I'm still single?" I asked.

Petunia laughed. "Are you saying you're not?"

Petunia walked back inside the building before I had a chance to answer. Miss May entered next, and I closed the door behind me and followed close behind.

As soon as we entered the backstage area, I noticed that we were surrounded by props from prior productions. There was a large painting of a sunset. Off in the corner, I spotted a life-size Frankenstein dummy. Sparkly costumes and top hats hung from dozens of pegs on the wall.

I looked around and my brow crinkled. "I'm confused. Petunia... Do you live here now?"

Petunia rolled her eyes. "Why would I live here? There is no nursing staff. No one makes your meals. Do you see a bed?"

I shrugged.

"You've been to my luxury retirement apartment at *Washington Villages*."

"I know," I conceded. "I'm just confused. If you don't live here... what are you doing here?"

"Petunia works at the theater on the weekends," Miss May said.

Petunia nodded. "I've been working here part-time for twenty plus years. So they gave me a key. When I started here I was a full three inches taller than I am now, believe it or not." *I believed it.* "Miss May said you needed a little help. She gives me free baked goods all the tooting time. One hand washes the other. Even though she's also accused me of murder. I forgive and forget. That gets easier the older you get."

"Thanks, Petunia," said Miss May. "I appreciate you meeting us here so late."

"I'm up all night, every night at the poker tables. Fleecing those old ladies. Making sure all the money in their estates goes to me instead of some snub-nosed grand-kid. This isn't late for me. It's the middle of the day."

Miss May chuckled. "Makes sense."

"So you two are here looking for a clue in this murder, right? Guy got shot right on stage. This is why I never attend the theater."

"But you work here..." I said.

"Ah, I like the pomp and circumstance. The costumes, the props, the sets. Plus, this is where I get my gambling money."

Miss May and I nodded. Petunia plopped down in a chair and opened a book about poker theory. "Go wherever you want but don't leave a trace. I don't need the cops breathing down my neck about colluding with the amateur detectives in town."

Miss May nodded. "No one will ever know we were here."

Miss May and I started off by looking around the stage where Adam had been shot. The police caution tape was still up. There was still a very clear mark where Adam had fallen. But there wasn't any other evidence up there. No bullets or shells or casings. The police had taken everything but the blood stain.

Next, Miss May insisted that she and I walk up and down every row in the theater. We started at the orchestra level and used our cell phones as flashlights. Miss May instructed me to pick up anything that might be suspicious. But it seemed the police had scoured the whole theater. I didn't find so much as a nickel of spare change or a stray piece of candy on the floor.

Finally, Miss May led the way up to the mezzanine level. "Remember. The shooter was probably stationed up here."

I approached the railing and looked down at the stage. It was hard to believe there had been so much creative energy on the stage the prior night. All that remained was a pervasive sense of doom and a gloomy pall. I couldn't look away from the spot where Adam had been shot. Somewhere deep down, I felt like if I looked hard enough, I might have the ability to turn back time. Like I was somehow going to be able to call out and warn Adam of his impending fate. I wanted so desperately to change the outcome of what had happened on that stage. But I couldn't.

Miss May approached and stood by my side. She let out a deep sigh. "I can't believe he was standing there saying his lines only hours ago. The guy may have been pompous, but if we went around shooting every actor with a pompous streak, we'd miss out on a lot of quality entertainment."

*Truer words were never spoken,* I thought.

I turned to Miss May. "Did you find anything up there?"

She shook her head. "One last stop before we go."

Miss May led me back to the room where we had met Petunia. Petunia had fallen asleep with her feet up on the desk and her poker book over her face. *Gave new meaning to the term "poker face,"* I thought.

Miss May held a finger to her lips and crept into the room. She scanned the area with intense focus. Then her gaze rested on a little green book that was on the desk, right beside Petunia's feet. Miss May tiptoed toward the desk one step at a time. I hung back and breathed as quietly as I could.

Finally, Miss May reached out and slid the book off the desk. She held the book up to me. Gold letters were stenciled on front. "Pine Grove community theater: sign-in book."

Miss May handed the book to me and I stepped outside, holding it close to my chest. Everyone who entered the building the prior night had signed their name in that book. So the killer's name was somewhere in there.

We just had to find out who it was. And why they'd wanted to hurt Adam Smith.

## 8

## TATERS AND TURTLES

We were the first customers inside Teeny's restaurant on Saturday morning. I expected Teeny to be happy to see us. But when we told her about our visit to the theater she looked disappointed.

"So you got nothing." Teeny shook her head. "I thought you two were experts. The top of the charts. Billboard's Hot 100."

"We are chart-toppers," said Miss May. "But there was nothing to find. The cops cleaned the place out."

Teeny rolled her eyes. "I don't believe you. The police in this town are so stupid. And they're not smart-stupid like Chelsea. They're stupid-stupid. There is no way they got all the clues from that theater."

"We got the sign-in book," I said.

Teeny turned and walked into the kitchen. "Who cares about the sign-in book?"

We followed her into the back.

Teeny grabbed a potato and gave it an angry peel. "Would you sign your name in a book if you were a killer?"

I chewed on my lower lip. "I guess not." I turned to Miss May. "We didn't think of that."

Miss May shrugged. "I thought about it. But I still think that sign-in book will come in handy."

"Red herring," said Teeny. "Classic case of red herring. What now? Question everyone in the entire book? Might as well question the whole town. Waste of time. Honestly."

"You're a tough critic this morning," said Miss May.

"Yeah," I said. "We snuck into the scene of the crime after-hours. In my book, that's pretty good."

Teeny tossed her potato down. "I know. I'm sorry. It's just... I'm tired. I had two people call in sick this morning. I have a hundred potatoes to peel, at least. And there's a crazed, highly-trained assassin on the loose."

Miss May stepped toward Teeny with a sympathetic look. "Hey. It's OK. The assassin might not be trained."

Teeny sighed. "Oh, well now I feel better. The worst part is, I should never take out these frustrations on the two of you. You were at the restaurant helping. And you're constantly braving danger in the name of justice. My only job is to peel potatoes and I can barely manage that."

"Teeny. That is so not true," I said. "You're not just a tater peeler. You're one of the sleuths."

Teeny looked up at me with big, wide eyes. "You mean that?"

I smiled. "Of course. You have been so important to all these investigations."

Miss May chuckled. "Is that what this is about? You're not feeling sleuth-y enough? Well that is ridiculous. You know we love you. You know you're important to these investigations. Get over yourself."

Miss May was a big believer in tough love. She was often stern with people she loved most.

Teeny nodded. "OK, alright, sounds good. You're just trying to be nice."

"She's not being nice," I said. "She just told you to get over yourself."

"Yeah, that's her way of being nice," Teeny said. "Anyway, I'm sorry I was negative. The sign-in book might be helpful. Even though I think it's unlikely the killer would have signed it."

Miss May tossed me a potato peeler. I got to work peeling. She did the same.

"So what do you think we should do, Teeny?"

"Try to get the knots out. I don't leave any flecks of skin. I like my hashbrowns pure."

Miss May shook her head. "Not with the potatoes. We know how to peel potatoes." *Speak for yourself.* "With the investigation."

Teeny nodded. "Oh. Now I understand.... I think we should go back to the suspects we discussed earlier. Dorothy was furious and there's no reason she couldn't have pulled the trigger."

I nodded. "Same with Master Skinner. I don't think he's a killer, but he seemed a little unhinged at *Peter's* the other night. Although if I were him I would kill with karate, not with a bullet."

Miss May shook her head. "Karate is sacred to Master Skinner. I don't think he would use it to kill."

"Is Skinner in the sign-in book?" Teeny asked.

I pulled the book from my purse and opened it. I scanned line by line with my pointer finger. "Doesn't look like it. But none of the actors are. Hold on one second."

I pulled out my smart phone and dialed Germany. He answered after the first ring. "Hi, Germany. Sorry. I know it's early."

"It's fine," he said. "Can I help with the investigation?"

Germany's tone was terse. Somehow I had forgotten that I have been short with him in the barn the prior night.

"Yeah. But..." I cast a look at Teeny and Miss May. They were watching me carefully. They sensed my unease. I walked back out into the dining area to continue the conversation.

"But what?" Germany asked.

"I'm sorry about last night. We're all feeling anxious about what happened."

Germany didn't say anything for a few seconds. "It's fine. I'm sorry, too. Thank you for understanding."

"I don't understand," I said. "I hope you're not going to carry on with the production of the play tonight."

"What did you want to ask me, Chelsea?"

"Did Master Skinner show up for the play last night?"

"He was there before curtains... But I didn't see him after."

I swallowed. "So it's possible..."

"Yes," said Germany. "It's possible Master Skinner killed Adam."

## 9

## ALARM BELLS WILL RING

*T*eeny, Miss May, and I walked over to Master Skinner's dojo in a hurry. Our faces were taut and and our hands were shoved in our pockets. Although growing up I had known Master Skinner as the calm, patient sensei who'd taught me all my sweet karate moves... I'd seen him blow his top a few times over the course of prior investigations. I didn't like treating my mentor as a suspect, but I also couldn't ignore facts. As we approached the dojo, I gulped quietly.

"That was a loud gulp, Chelsea," said Teeny.

*Maybe not as quietly as I thought.* I looked at Teeny. "Master Skinner is tough. I feel like I'm gonna pee my pants."

"Me too," Teeny said. "But also, I chugged a bunch of coffee so I actually have to pee."

Miss May gave me a dismissive wave of the hand. "We'll be fine. Master Skinner is calm and reasonable."

"Most of the time that's true," said Teeny. "But if he's the killer... He'll karate chop his way to freedom no matter what. Unless the student has what it takes to overcome the teacher..."

"I...might?" I said, not wanting to imagine a throwdown with the master himself.

"Whatever the case may be, we're almost there," Miss May said. "Let's take some deep breaths and try to keep it together."

Teeny nodded. "Alright. I'll stay calm. I mean, Chelsea has at least 50/50 odds of beating Master Skinner in a fight, right?"

I shook my head. "Not sure. Master Skinner could probably take me even if he had both arms tied behind his back."

"For sure," Miss May said. "That man doesn't need arms to beat you in a fight. He has those strong little legs. He could donkey kick you right through the wall."

"That's not reassuring," I said. "I thought you wanted us to stay calm!"

"I do," Miss May said. "Because I brought my own secret weapon." Miss May held open her purse. Inside, there was a freshly baked apple pie.

Miss May's pies often came in handy during investigations. As soon as suspects were plied with a homemade pie, they tended to relax and open up. I hoped Skinner liked pies, but I wasn't so sure.

"No offense," I said. "But I don't think that pie's going to help. Master Skinner is above most earthly temptations. Unless maybe he helps himself to a slice after beating us all up."

Teeny thrust her pointer finger into the air. "My thoughts exactly. Why are we interviewing a trained martial artist right off the bat? We should have started with Dorothy."

Miss May shrugged. "We're here now. So let's go inside."

Miss May reached out and tugged on the door handle. It didn't open. "That's weird. It's locked."

Miss May cupped her hands and peered inside the dojo. "Master Skinner usually runs classes from 8 AM until 5 PM on Saturdays."

I nodded. "It's his busiest day of the week. Are you sure the door is locked?" I tugged on the door too. Yup. Locked alright.

I cupped my hands over my eyes and looked inside. So did Teeny. Sure enough, the place was dark. The mats were stacked up against the walls. The back wall, lined with Master Skinner's karate trophies, looked sinister in the dimly lit dojo. I shuddered. "I forgot how many trophies he has."

Teeny swallowed. "Terrifying. I wonder how many of those were awarded specifically for a killer donkey kick?"

Miss May stepped away from the window and crossed her arms. "OK. This is suspicious. It's very unlike Master Skinner to close the dojo."

"Chelsea, you said Germany was considering running the play tonight, right?" Teeny asked. "Maybe Skinner is home preparing for his role, now that he's the lead."

"I don't know. Germany seemed pretty determined to put on the show, but I'm not sure if he'll go through with it," I said.

"I hope he doesn't," said Miss May. "But you're right. Skinner is probably home preparing."

Teeny took a step toward the parking lot. "So let's go talk to him at his house."

Miss May took Teeny's arm and pulled her back. "Not so fast. If the dojo is empty maybe we can go inside and take a look."

I glanced up and down the street. No one was in sight. "You want to break into Master Skinner's dojo?"

Miss May shrugged. "I want to investigate. Just for a few minutes." Miss May turned to Teeny. "Remember when this place used to be Gina's hair salon?"

Teeny nodded. "How could I forget? That girl gave me ten of the worst haircuts of my life."

"Why did you keep going back?" I asked.

"I loved Gina. She was hysterical. And I didn't want to hurt her feelings."

Miss May nodded. "She really was funny. I went just for the gossip. Terrible haircuts, though. Makes sense she went out of business."

"OK," I said. "But why is that relevant now?"

Miss May touched her nose. "Back when Gina owned this place she lost the keys to the front door. But she never bothered getting a new set because the door was in such bad condition, when she jiggled the handle it popped right open."

Teeny smiled. "And you think Master Skinner never fixed the door?"

Miss May shrugged. "It's worth a shot."

I smiled. "Small-town life never ceases to amaze me."

"Let's see if this works, then you can be amazed." Miss May grabbed the door handle and jiggled. She jiggled harder and harder. My amazement was starting to fade when voila! The door opened.

Miss May turned back to me with a grin. "I knew it."

Then... Beep. Beep. Beep.

The lights of a security alarm flashed inside the dojo. A loud voice boomed from a speaker on the wall. "Intruder. Intruder. Leave immediately."

Miss May, Teeny, and I stumbled back out to the sidewalk. Miss May pulled the door closed and the alarm immediately turned off. The three of us breathed a collective sigh of relief.

Miss May pressed her palms to her chest. "Wow. That was close."

A deep, male voice boomed from behind us. "You're telling me."

We turned. There was Detective Wayne Hudson. He looked tall. Strapping. Handsome, as always.

But he did not look happy.

## 10

## WAYNE'S WORLD

"*Y*ou got here fast," I said.

"The police are taking a very active role in the community these days," said Wayne. "Vigorous patrolling."

Miss May cocked her head. "Glad to hear it. But are you sure you didn't just happen to be walking by? That cup of coffee you're holding from the *Brown Cow* is so hot it's still steaming. Tells me you were in the neighborhood."

Wayne raised his eyebrows. "Maybe I was testing your detective skills, Miss May. Nice job. I was walking by."

"Want to know what else gave you away?" I asked.

Wayne smirked. "Sure. Tell me."

"You're wearing blue jeans."

"Are you saying you like my pants?" Wayne raised a flirtatious eyebrow. OK, maybe his eyebrow wasn't flirtatious. But in my mind, it was.

"I'm saying when you're working you wear slacks, that's all."

Wayne leaned forward to look in my eyes. I tried not to

blink. His blue-green eyes were mesmerizing, and I felt for a moment like I was under the spell of a hypnotist.

"Chelsea is with Germany now," said Teeny. "Have you seen them around town? They're such a cute couple."

*Germany. Right. My boyfriend.* I blinked and looked away from Wayne's piercing gaze.

"Of course Wayne has seen them together," said Miss May. "It's a small town."

"OK," said Teeny. "Good to see you, Detective. Have a nice day."

Teeny took a step as if to go around Wayne. He blocked her path. "Not so fast, ladies. We have still have the issue of a certain dojo alarm to discuss."

Miss May nodded. "Oh, right. The alarm. Yeah. We heard it and we walked right over from Teeny's restaurant. Got here before you did, in fact."

Wayne narrowed his eyes. "So you didn't cause the alarm? You swear?"

I scoffed. "Of course not. Why would we want to get inside Master Skinner's dojo? It is suspicious that he's not there today, sure, and he was really mad about not being the lead in the play, yeah. But he's probably just sleeping in... Because... Everyone knows Master Skinner loves to sleep." I cringed. *Classic Chelsea babble.*

"Classic Chelsea babble," Wayne said. "We all know Skinner is a suspect in this murder."

Teeny turned down the sides of her mouth. "I don't know that. I don't know anything. Wait. Someone was murdered?"

Wayne rolled his eyes. "Look. You're right. I wasn't here when the alarm went off. I was getting coffee. So I can't bring you in on breaking and entering." Wayne peered around Miss May to get a look inside the dojo. "And the place looks untouched so I don't feel the need to investigate further. But if Chief Flanagan were the one walking by today, with a fresh, steaming hot cup of coffee? She wouldn't let you off so easy."

"I don't know what you're talking about," said Miss May.

Wayne nodded. "I'm sure you don't. I'm sure you don't have a fresh pie in your purse that you planned to use for bribing Master Skinner. And I'm sure you have no idea what I mean when I say you need to stay out of this investigation. Right?"

Miss May offered her best doe-eyed stare. "I don't know what you mean."

"Right. So let's skip that whole dance. I'm not a good dancer anyway. Right, Chelsea?"

I stammered. Wayne was a great dancer. And yes, once upon a time, Wayne and I had shared a romantic waltz in the event barn. And yes, I had wanted to date him for a while, and being in his arms felt safe and— *Whoops, getting distracted.*

"As far as I recall, you've got two left feet," I said.

Wayne chuckled. He stepped aside and gestured with a sweep of his arm to let us pass. "You three should get on your way. Try not to set off any more alarms on your journey. Remember... Most cops aren't as nice as I am."

Miss May, Teeny, and I edged past Wayne. I could smell his earthy, cinnamon cologne as I stepped past him back onto Commerce Street. I was thankful, at least that time, that Wayne had decided to let us go.

## 11

## SORRY, CHARLIE

*M*aster Skinner lived in a split-level ranch just around the corner from the Pine Grove Elementary School. Although Skinner was a bachelor, the place was well-maintained. There were window boxes in every window. A crisp American flag hung from the porch. And the mailbox was hand-painted with the image of a karate master meditating.

The mid-morning sun flooded the well-kept lawn as Miss May, Teeny, and I approached. Although it was late March, and spring was around the corner, the air was still cool and the ground was still muddy and squishy under my feet. I shoved my hands in my pockets, ready for April to come — hopefully without more showers.

"Master Skinner's house is so cute," I said. "Not at all the minimalist design I'd expect from a karate bachelor."

Teeny nodded. "The man has great taste and an enormous attention to detail. I heard he painted the mailbox himself."

Miss May shook her head. "I heard the Johnson widow painted it for him for his birthday."

Teeny's eyes widened. "Really? Were they an item?"

"Not officially. But I heard from several sources that she paid him visits late at night and then again early in the morning."

Teeny chuckled. "You know everything that goes on in this town."

Miss May shot Teeny a look. "You were my source! You were the one who told me all that!"

Teeny laughed. "I was? I forget how much I know sometimes. I hear so much gossip, some of it's bound to go in one ear and get lost on its way out of my mouth."

"Me too," said Miss May.

"Me three. But between the two of you, there are very few secrets in Pine Grove."

Miss May nodded. "If only we knew who killed Adam Smith, we might know everything." My aunt turned to me. "Are you feeling OK? Or are you still nervous about the potential donkey kick?"

I shrugged. "It's weird... I feel better. After leaving the dojo, I don't know, I feel less stressed. I don't know why."

Miss May looked at me over her glasses. "I know why."

I shook my head. "It has nothing to do with Wayne."

"Sure it doesn't," said Teeny. "Who would feel safe around a big, burly police officer? Not me."

I stammered. "OK, fine. Maybe I feel a little better knowing that Wayne is patrolling the streets. But that's not because of my semi-romantic history with him. It's because I'm glad to know Pine Grove has at least one decent police officer."

"Decent is generous," said Miss May. "We solved every murder before him. Don't forget that."

Miss May rang Master Skinner's doorbell. "Master Skinner. It's Chelsea, Teeny, and Miss May. Are you home?"

I whispered. "Miss May. You're just going to call out and announce us like that?"

"We're just delivering a pie, Chelsea. Nothing to be weird about."

"She is still scared about the donkey kick," said Teeny.

Miss May chuckled. Teeny chuckled right along with her. I glowered at the both of them.

Ten seconds later, and the front door opened. There stood Master Skinner. But he wasn't wearing his typical gi. Instead, he was dressed like a southern gentleman, wearing a cotton suit with a straw hat. And he had a pipe in his mouth.

"Master Skinner," I said, startled. "You look like you're ready for a performance of...something."

Master Skinner replied in a slow, southern drawl. "Now I'm not quite sure I know of which play you speak, young lady. I'm just living my life down here in beautiful Charleston, South Carolina. There's trouble afoot but I'm an honest man and I'm determined to make an honest living."

I glanced over at Teeny and Miss May. They both looked like they were holding in laughter.

"Hi, Master Skinner," said Teeny.

Master Skinner chastised Teeny with a stern tone. "I do not know any Master Skinner. I'm a simple, southern man."

Miss May leaned over and whispered loudly enough for me to hear. "I think he's in character for the play."

"Oh," I said. "Of course. But the play might not even happen. And also...there's no Southern gentleman in *Phantom.*"

"All I know is that there will be a great performance in the high school auditorium this evening. That's right," Skinner said, in response to our shocked faces. "I was just informed by my friend, Germany. It's official."

"Hold on," I said. "Germany made the decision? He's going ahead with the play tonight?"

"I'm but a simple southern gentleman," Skinner reiterated. "But I have heard of a performance in the high school auditorium."

"I'm confused," said Teeny. "Will someone please explain to me what's going on?"

"Master Skinner is in character for the play tonight. He doesn't want to break character so he's acting like a southern gentleman for some reason, even though, like Chelsea said, the play is *Phantom of the Opera*. But he also wants us to go see him in the play...so he's telling us that it's in the high school auditorium instead of the theater where the murder happened," said Miss May. Miss May turned to Master Skinner. "Is that right?"

Master Skinner shrugged. "I'm sorry. I was just sitting down for tea. If you'd like to join me, that would be wonderful. Otherwise, you all best be on your way."

Miss May smiled. "We'd love to join you."

Master Skinner led us out to his back porch, where a gallon of sweet tea waited. He grabbed a few cups from the kitchen, filled them up with tea, and we all sat down.

"So, Master Skinner," said Miss May.

Master Skinner held up his hand. "Call me Charlie. Charlie is my name."

Miss May shot me a confused look and continued. "OK, Charlie. We're here to talk to you about the death of Adam Smith."

Master Skinner shook his head. "I was so saddened to hear of that tragedy. Terrible thing. Violence is never the answer. That's what my little mama always said."

"That's ironic coming from the man with the infamous donkey kick," said Teeny.

Master Skinner glared. "What was that?"

Teeny sat straight up. "Nothing. Nevermind, Charlie."

"Pardon me," I said, unable to contain myself, "but is Germany putting on a different play? I'm just confused because the lead in *Phantom of the Opera* is not a Southern gentleman named Charlie."

"I have never heard of this *Phantom*," Master Skinner said. "I am but a humble Southern boy who rarely got to the thee-ater."

I stared at Master Skinner, baffled but impressed by his commitment. *I guess everyone has their methods.*

"Anyway," said Miss May. "We wanted to talk to you. See, we heard that the police suspect our friend Master Skinner of the murder. In fact, we saw Detective Wayne Hudson at Master Skinner's dojo this morning. Snooping around." *So much for just delivering a pie.*

Master Skinner choked on his sweet tea. "Is that right? I do declare. Please, continue with your tale."

I nodded and picked up where Miss May had left off. "That's right. Detective Hudson was at the dojo. He was suspicious. And it seemed like he wanted to arrest Master Skinner."

Master Skinner pounded his fist on the table. "Arrest? That is absurd. I believe I've met this Master Skinner, once or twice. Terrific fellow. And very tall."

Teeny scoffed. "Master Skinner is not tall."

Master Skinner glared. Teeny gulped. "He's very tall. Master Skinner is a giant. Who am I to talk? People who live in short houses, am I right?"

"So you came by my humble abode to gossip about police activity?" Charlie drawled.

Miss May shook her head. "We were looking for Master Skinner. We thought he might be here. We didn't want to gossip. But we thought it would be prudent to let him know he was a suspect."

Master Skinner shook his head. "These police are ridiculous. Who would suspect a gallant, very tall, local business leader like Master Skinner of murder?"

"I would suspect him," said Teeny. "He always seemed a little crazy to me. And he's got an untrustworthy face. Plus, everyone knows he was hooking up with the Johnson widow. And I think he broke her heart. Which is not very nice."

Master Skinner stood with such force that he knocked his chair over. "That's enough gossip in my home." Impressively, he didn't break his Southern character at all.

Miss May held up her hands. "We're not gossiping. We're sorry. Teeny, tell Charlie you're sorry."

Teeny nodded. "I'm sorry. I really am. Your acting is so good. I forgot that you're not Charlie."

"I am Charlie."

"Right." Teeny rubbed her head. "I'm sorry. I'm confused."

Master Skinner turned backwards and donkey kicked the back door open. It almost exploded off the hinges. "You may leave now."

Miss May, Teeny, and I hurried out. Master Skinner's face reddened as we exited. "Never speak ill of Master Skinner again. You hear me? Or you'll have to answer to Charlie!"

"Sorry, Charlie," Teeny called back.

Master Skinner slammed the door and disappeared inside his house.

I looked back at Master Skinner's house before I climbed into Miss May's VW bus. Master Skinner glared at us from the front window. I didn't want to think that Master Skinner was guilty.

But the whole Charlie routine was unsettling. And if Skinner was the killer, then I feared Adam would not be his last victim in Pine Grove.

## 12

## EWING AIN'T SEEN NOTHING YET

*M*iss May, Teeny, and I hurried out of Master Skinner's house in a disoriented frenzy.

Teeny darted out in front of us, running at full speed with her hands above her head. "Start the car. He's out of his mind."

Miss May dug around in her purse. "I can't find my keys."

"He's going to donkey kick us without even spilling his sweet tea," said Teeny. "Which was delicious, by the way."

"Talk about the sweet tea later." I pointed at Miss May's belt. "The keys are clipped to your pants."

Miss May unclipped the keys from her pants with a sigh of relief. She unlocked the VW bus and we piled in.

"Drive faster," said Teeny.

"We don't need to be in a hurry anymore," said Miss May. "We're in the van. We got away."

"I know." Teeny buckled her seatbelt. "But now I'm hungry."

Miss May laughed and took a hard left turn. "We're right near *Ewing's Eats*."

Teeny rubbed her tiny hands together. "I'm well aware. Now let's see how fast this baby can go."

Minutes later, the three of us were seated at a picnic table outside *Ewing's Eats*. *Ewing's* was a little burger shack outside of Pine Grove. The eponymous proprietor was one of the nicest guys in town. He gave us each a burger and fries for free but he made Teeny pay for her chocolate milkshake with triple sprinkles. I think just because he got a kick out of seeing her pout.

Mr. Ewing smiled as he approached and placed the food on our picnic table. "There you go, ladies. You enjoy, now."

Miss May smiled. "We always do."

"Hey," said Mr. Ewing. "Are you three working on solving the case of the actor's assassination?"

"Ohhh alliterative case title, I like it," Teeny said.

"Thanks," Mr. Ewing said. "You think you're gonna figure out who killed him?"

Miss May popped a fry in her mouth. "That's the plan."

Mr. Ewing looked down and picked at his nails. "Do you think if you have any important breakthroughs here at my restaurant... Will you mention it to the newspapers?"

"We might have accommodated your request, if somebody didn't have to pay for her triple sprinkle milkshake," said Teeny, crossing her arms.

Miss May side-eyed Teeny, then looked over to Mr. Ewing. "Of course we'll mention it. You don't need to give us food for free."

"It's the least I could do," said Mr. Ewing. "Just mention me in the newspaper! Always looking for ways to drum up business. And if someone snaps and murders me one day? Will you three find out who did it?"

Miss May shook her head. "No one is going to murder you, Patrick. You're the nicest guy in town."

I nodded. "And you make the best fries in New York State."

Mr. Ewing grinned. "I don't know. I have a few enemies. Teeny here seemed pretty miffed when I charged her for that milkshake."

"Oh, I'm miffed alright," Teeny said, "but not murderin' miffed. That's a whole different category."

"Well that's a relief," Ewing said, and strode back toward his restaurant.

"Nice guy," said Teeny. "I hope he didn't just jinx himself into getting murdered."

Miss May nodded. "We all do."

"Do you think there's anyone in town who might want to hurt him?" Teeny took a sip of her milkshake.

"I think we should solve the actual murder of Adam Smith before we solve the hypothetical murder of Patrick Ewing," I said.

Teeny rolled her eyes. "Fine. Although there's not much left to solve. Charlie did it."

Miss May took a bite of her burger. "You mean Master Skinner."

Teeny scooted to the edge of her seat. "He had tons of motive. He's taking over Adam's role in the play. And he's clearly excited about the opportunity. Plus, his fists and donkey legs are lethal."

"Too bad we got ushered out before we could really talk to him," I said.

"He was in a hurry for us to leave." Miss May wiped her mouth with a napkin. "Much less calm and collected than usual. And relatively uncooperative."

"Uncooperative is a generous word for what Master Skinner pulled in there." Teeny grabbed the spoon and plunged it into her milkshake. "He was pretending to be an old Southern gentleman for the entire conversation."

"That's true," I said, giggling at the memory. "Sorry. I know murder's not funny. But my karate teacher doing a Southern accent just makes me laugh. Still, Master Skinner's method acting is still pretty far from an admission of guilt. Master Skinner has always been eccentric."

The three of us ate in silence for a few moments. I took a deep breath of the crisp spring air. Birds chirped in a tree above me. An old pickup truck rattled by on the road.

I shook my head. "But then again, I don't think we can rule Master Skinner out as a suspect. Germany can't verify that Skinner was backstage at the time of the shooting. Plus, there are no southern gentleman in the *Phantom of the Opera*. Maybe the sensei lost his mind."

Miss May nodded. "Sure, that's possible. But we need to talk to someone other than Skinner if we want any information."

Teeny sat up. "Petunia was working the door at the theater last night, right?"

Miss May nodded. "Good idea. Let's talk to Petunia. Maybe she saw Master Skinner."

I ate my last fry. "I hope she did. For better or worse."

## 13

## KISS MY PETUNIAS

*T*he *Washington Villages* retirement community was unlike anywhere else in Pine Grove. It was built in the early 2000s, so it lacked the historical character and architecture compared to many of the buildings in our small town. I wouldn't say the construction was cheap, but from a design perspective it was homogenous and lacked any sense of respect for its surroundings.

The buildings were all identical, with white vinyl siding and perfect little squares of grass in front of each one — like a computer-simulated world created by a very unimaginative mind.

Bland architecture aside, there was a lot of activity at *Washington Villages*. Tennis courts occupied the center of the complex. A big clubhouse near the entrance advertised BINGO and other entertainment. On any given day, the place was teeming with Pine Grove's hottest, sexiest residents aged 55 and over. Shirtless men in their 70's pumped iron, bikini-clad octogenarians sunned poolside, and of course, Petunia ran her infamous poker games every night from 10 PM until dawn.

That day, we entered the back room to find Petunia in the middle of an intense game of Texas Hold 'Em. I wasn't sure if she was starting early or ending late, but either way, she looked like she'd been in the exact same position for at least twenty-four hours.

Petunia sat at a felt table with six other elderly women. A green visor perched on her curly hair. She chomped on the end of a number two pencil like it was a Cuban cigar. Petunia was a small woman with a big personality. She ran her card games like a Vegas hustler, and seeing her in her element was a dark thrill — like seeing a velociraptor on the hunt.

"It's on you, Ethel. You want to raise me?" Petunia growled. "I've got position on you. Not a smart move. If you double my bet, I'm pushing all in. For better or for worse. So I hope you're ready to blow your whole stack."

Petunia glared across the table at Ethel, her good friend and poker enemy. Ethel was a little hard of hearing and a lot bad at poker, so she was the perfect patsy for Petunia's card shark skills.

Ethel cupped her hand to her ear. "What?"

"I said if you raise me, I'm going all in." Petunia shook her head. "It's on you."

Another woman at the table picked up a novel and began to read quietly to herself. Clearly, she was used to a slow pace of play.

"Come on. Somebody's gonna fall asleep or kick the bucket if you don't make a move soon! Place your bet or..." Petunia took the pencil out of her mouth. "...or you can't play for a week."

Ethel laid her hand down on the table. "I fold. I have to go to the bathroom." Ethel pushed her chair back and hobbled out of the room. Petunia glanced over her shoulder and noticed me, Teeny, and Miss May. "Oh great. It's Pine Grove's most unlikely trio of detectives. I know you took my sign-in sheet."

Petunia's ability to read people at the card table clearly carried over into real life. I smiled. "None of us know anything about any sign-in sheet."

Petunia collected the chips from the middle of the table and began to deal a new hand. "It's fine. I just worked there. If you girls think you need it for evidence, whatever. But it's not like I'm a diligent bookkeeper at that theater. They don't pay me enough."

A little old lady spoke up from across the poker table. "You volunteer."

"They give me free tickets and unlimited *Raisinets*, OK? Mind your own business. You want me to kick you out of the game?"

The little old lady cowered. "Apologies. Don't kick me out. I love my cards. I love my puzzles and I love my cards."

Petunia shook her head. "No one is talking about puzzles. You know what? Let's take five, ladies. I'll deal with these silly detectives and I'll be right back."

Petunia strutted across the room and got a drink from the water fountain. She wiped her mouth as she turned back to us. "You want to find out if I saw something suspicious in the theater that night? Of course I did. Every actor in that play hated one another. And Master Skinner has come unhinged."

Teeny leaned in. "So you've met Charlie?"

Petunia scoffed. "Everyone in town has met Charlie. You just met Charlie? I thought you three knew everything?"

Miss May shrugged. "It seems we know less than we think. That's why we need to talk to you. You're one of our most reliable sources."

Petunia nodded. "I have incredible skills of observation. I was almost a fighter pilot."

I cocked my head in skepticism but before I could question Petunia's claim, Miss May piped up. "That doesn't surprise me one bit. Look at you now. You're a wizard at the poker table. A regular card counting genius."

Petunia shook her head. "Card counting is blackjack. I play poker. The game is Texas Hold 'Em. No limit. Pure aggression. Pure people-reading. My job at the table is to pick out the weakest woman and take her for all she's worth."

I hung my head. "Poor Ethel."

"No. Not poor Ethel," Petunia said. "She chooses to come back to the tables. It's better her money goes to me that some snot-nosed brat who's going to waste his inheritance."

"Right," I said. "I think you mentioned snot-nosed kids at the theater."

Miss May loudly ahemed. "We're getting off topic. I have more questions for you. Do you think that Master Skinner is a real suspect? Did you see him go upstairs? Do you think he was in the mezzanine?"

Petunia laughed. "Master Skinner didn't shoot Adam Smith."

Miss May looked around then looked back at Petunia. "Who did?"

Teeny stepped forward. "Was it Dorothy? When Adam kissed Zambia onstage... Dorothy looked angry enough to kill. And I don't blame her."

Petunia shook her head. "Forget Dorothy. She's a lamb. A cute little jealous lamb. Defenseless. In fact, I should recruit her to play in my poker game. You need to talk to Zambia."

Miss May rubbed her chin. "Why? She was the one kissing Adam. It seems like that's what she wanted."

"Zambia wanted Dorothy to leave Adam. She was tired of sharing the man with his wife. But Adam kept making promises and... Well, he was still married."

Miss May's eyes widened. "That is hot gossip, Petunia."

Petunia smiled, proud. "I told you. I know everything. Yeah, sure. Master Skinner went up to the mezzanine. But this Zambia motive makes way more sense."

I narrowed my eyes. "Wait, what?"

Petunia nodded. "Yeah, you heard me right. Skinner went up to the mezzanine. But I just don't think it was him. Like I said, Dorothy, Zambia, and Adam had a fiery love triangle and I'd bet my last three nights' winnings that one of those women murdered him."

Miss May sighed. "Nonetheless. Why did Skinner go up to the mezzanine? We need to go back and have a word with Charlie."

A frail, female voice rang out from behind us. "No you don't." We turned to see the little old lady Petunia had scolded at the card table. She'd clearly been eavesdropping. "I know where Skinner was last night. Follow me and I'll tell you everything I know."

## 14

## PAINT BY MURDERS

*W*e followed the old woman about two hundred feet to her apartment. The short walk took about fifteen minutes, and I kept feeling the urge to just pick the little lady up and carry her the rest of the way. The little woman entered her apartment and flicked on the lights. I looked around. To my right was a large dining room table. The dining room bled into a small TV room with a couch and armchair. A sliding glass door looked out to a pond. The walls were decorated with decades of family photos.

The little old woman sat at the dining room table and gestured for the three of us to sit across from her.

"Hello," she said. "My name is Wendy Johnson. And what I'm about to tell you can never leave this room."

Miss May sat. Teeny and I took the seats on either side of her. It was a tight fit on the small couch, but we were comfortable enough with each other to overlap a little.

Miss May gave Wendy a solemn nod. "Of course. You have our word. Right ladies?"

"Yep," I said.

"Word," Teeny said.

"You're surprised we've never met," said Wendy, focusing on Miss May.

Miss May nodded thoughtfully. "I suppose I am. Pine Grove is a small place."

Teeny leaned forward. "And the three of us get around. You know, in the non-sexy sense."

Wendy nodded. "I've been living here in *Washington Villages* for many, many years. I'm older than I look."

I bit my tongue. The lady looked ancient. She must have been a hundred and thirty.

"You look pretty old," said Teeny. She smiled. "We all do, except for Chelsea. We're always complaining about her youth."

Wendy tilted her head back and let out a slow, rumbling laugh. It had the same steady determination that I heard in her speaking voice. "If you're not jealous of young people you must not be alive. That's what I always say."

"I'm sure even the dead are jealous of the young," Teeny said. I cast a sideways look at her. Sometimes, Teeny said some profound things — often unintentionally.

Miss May put her elbows on her knees. "What is it you want to tell us, Wendy? Why'd you bring us to your lovely home?"

Wendy sat back. "My son was William Johnson. He passed almost ten years ago."

Teeny's jaw dropped. "Oh. And he left his wife behind, did he?"

Wendy nodded. "Daisy Johnson. Wonderful woman. But very private."

I looked over at Teeny and Miss May, trying to piece things together. Earlier that day, Miss May and Teeny had mentioned something about Master Skinner taking up with the Johnson widow. It seemed that widow was named Daisy Johnson. Wendy was her mother-in-law. Wendy claimed to have information pertaining to Master Skinner's where-abouts on the night of the murder. So I assumed she was about to tell us that Daisy and Master Skinner were indeed an item. I was wrong.

"I know what you're thinking," said Wendy. "But you're wrong. The rumor mill chews up Pine Grove's most whole-some citizens and grinds them into tasty lies. Daisy hasn't been with a man since William passed. She's devoted her life to watercolor painting, in fact. She's found a lot of solace in her art."

Miss May narrowed her eyes. "I'm sorry. If there was no, uh, intimacy... I'm struggling to see the connection between Master Skinner and your daughter-in-law, the watercolor painter."

Wendy sighed. "Daisy and Master Skinner did have something of a relationship. And they were together last night. But their liaisons are purely professional."

Teeny leaned forward so far it looked like she was about to topple into a new plane of existence. "Tell us, Wendy. What are you talking about?"

Wendy hesitated. "You promised to never share this information with anyone."

Miss May nodded. "Absolutely. Whatever you're about to tell us will remain a secret forever."

Wendy took a deep breath. "OK. Master Skinner is Daisy's model."

Teeny laughed in disbelief. "What? Are you telling me that she paints him?"

Wendy nodded. "There's something about him she finds incredibly inspiring. He's her muse. His icy-cold glare. His powerful, karate body... It inspires her."

Miss May blinked three times, with slow deliberation. "Are you telling me... Master Skinner is a nude model for the Johnson widow?"

Wendy gasped. "No. Not naked. He wears all his clothes. Sometimes his shorts are a bit shorter than what I find appropriate, at least that's what I think based on her portraits."

Teeny scrunched up her face. "If he's got his shirt and his short-shorts on, then why are these Skinner sessions such a secret?"

Wendy turned up her nose. "Because if anyone knew all the hours that Master Skinner spent at Daisy's home, people would talk. They wouldn't stop talking."

I shook my head. "Hold on a second. Master Skinner left in the middle of the play last night so Daisy Johnson could paint him?"

Wendy shrugged. "That's right. The man loves being a subject. He loves how much concentration it takes to stay still. Says it's meditative. Daisy had been asking him to pose for a new portrait for months. But he'd had to turn her down, over and over, to go to rehearsal. The night of the premier, Skinner was so frustrated, so angry at that ridiculous director and star... He left the theater and went straight to Daisy. Asked her to paint 'his angry face.' Wanted his emotion to be artistically useful in one way or another, I guess."

Miss May shook her head. "That is unbelievable. But I believe you."

Teeny sighed. "But if Skinner didn't kill Adam Smith, who did?"

"I agree with Petunia," said Wendy. "You need to talk to Zambia. And you need to do it sooner rather than later."

## 15

## ON GREENISH POND

*M*iss May, Teeny, and I left *Washington Villages* and headed over to Zambia's house. Zambia lived near Hastings Pond in the community that was originally designed as a summer getaway for New York City residents in the 50's. Our investigations had often brought us to Hastings Ponds — to visit local architect Sudeer Patel, or local hairstylist-turned-yogi Jennifer Paul, or really any local residents who were also murder suspects.

A large, somewhat greenish pond was the focal point of the community and dozens of cute, small cottages surround the water. Hastings Pond had thrived for decades after it was first built, but it fell into disrepair during my childhood. But young families started to move into the neighborhood because of its affordable access to good schools, and now the "lakeside housing" was part of an up-and-coming area in Pine Grove.

Seeing the pond reminded me that the three of us were good amateur detectives. We'd been at this for a while now, and we'd never failed. I felt a surge of confidence.

"We're good at this," I said. "The three of us. We always catch the killer."

Teeny clucked her tongue. "Don't jinx us, Chels!"

Miss May craned her head back to look at me. "Teeny's right. We are talented sleuths. But we can't start feeling too confident. The stakes are too high for us to make any arrogant errors."

*So much for confidence.* But I knew Miss May was right. Every time we went to someone's house, it was a coin toss... would we be interviewing a harmless garden snake, or a deadly viper ready to strike and kill? "You're right," I said. "Thanks for the reminder."

Miss May glanced at me in the rearview mirror. We made eye contact. She smiled. "If my niece wasn't so good at karate I'd be much more worried."

I chuckled. I wasn't that great at martial arts, but adrenaline seemed to amplify my abilities in a useful way. I'd used a kick or a chop in a lot of our suspect showdowns, and that made me proud. *Confidence, back.*

Zambia lived in a small, Cape Cod-style cottage right along the shore. Her house was gray with yellow detailing along the windows. A small chimney poked out of the roof like the end of the cigar. The place felt like it could be in a fairytale. The only question was... What kind of fairytale? And how did it end?

Miss May parked our yellow VW bus on the curb. Zambia was already on her driveway, lugging a rolling suitcase toward her maroon Honda Civic. She was dressed in a long, flowing gown. Her hair was pinned in an elaborate updo and her skin looked dewy and sparkly in the light.

Teeny gasped. "Oh my goodness. She's making her escape. We got here just in time."

Miss May turned down the sides of her mouth. "I don't think Zambia is going too far dressed like that."

"Why not?" Teeny said "If I were her I would want to look glamorous during my great escape. Otherwise, what's the point? You can't wear sweatpants to make a getaway."

I shook my head. "She's probably headed into town for the second production of the play. Pretty sure she's wearing her costume."

Teeny rolled her eyes. "That's what she wants you to think."

Miss May opened her door and hopped out. "Let's talk to her. See what we can find out."

Zambia popped the trunk of her car and heaved the small suitcase inside. "Go away. I don't want to talk to any of you. I don't care how many apple pies you have stashed in your purse, or how nice you pretend to be."

Clearly, Zambia had heard of Miss May's wily ways. The actress closed her trunk with a thud and stomped toward the car door.

Miss May held up her hands and spoke in a calm, warm tone. "I understand. And we're sorry to bombard you like this."

Zambia snorted at Miss May. "You think you're cool because you run around Pine Grove solving murders? You're nosy and rude. You accuse innocent people of murder and you ruin their reputations. Don't come anywhere near me."

"Your reputation is already ruined," said Teeny. She clapped her hand over her mouth. "Did I say that out loud? Oopsy-daisy."

Zambia growled at us, "Go. Away." She climbed behind the wheel of her car and slammed her door.

Miss May looked over at Teeny. "Why did you say that?"

Teeny winced. "Not my finest moment. And I've had a

lot of not fine moments. Listen, sometimes me and Chelsea just have a case of foot-in-mouth disease."

"Don't drag me down with you!" I protested. "I haven't said anything."

Miss May took a deep breath and crossed in front of Zambia's car to block Zambia's path from the driveway to the road. "I'm sorry," Miss May yelled over the hum of the engine. "Please. Give us five minutes of your time."

Zambia laid on the horn. Miss May plugged her ears. Zambia did not stop honking for at least twenty seconds. My hearing buds started to lose all sense of reality. *I know, I know, hearing buds aren't a thing. But you know what I mean.*

When the honking finally stopped, Miss May spoke. "We're not here to accuse you of anything. One quick conversation and you can be on your way."

Zambia shook her head. She put the car in reverse, did a little three-point turn, and drove across her front yard and onto the street. Seconds later, she had disappeared around the corner and was gone from our sight.

"Zambia's not one to be slowed down by roadblocks, I guess," I said.

Miss May trudged back toward the VW bus. "Come on."

Teeny and I exchanged a confused look.

"Where are we going?" I asked.

Miss May sighed. "We're going to enjoy a night out at the theater."

## 16

## LOONY TUNES

*T*he community theater was the site of an active crime scene investigation, so the play couldn't be hosted there that night. Instead, Germany had convinced the local high school to rent out their auditorium for the performance. The stage at the high school was smaller, but it was the only other option in town. Germany was lucky that the superintendent agreed on such short notice. A student's solo flute performance had been cancelled to allow for *Phantom* to use the space, but nobody, even the flautist herself, seemed too upset.

There were only five or six cars in the high school parking lot when we arrived. A gray mist hung in the air. The American flag, hung at half-mast in memory of our local Broadway hero, waved vigorously in a gust of wind. Yellow streetlights cast an eerie glow over the ground.

Miss May parked in a spot right out front. "Easy parking when everyone in town is too scared to see the play."

Teeny shrugged. "Works for me. If no one came to see the play tonight that means there won't be a line at the candy counter I can take my time deciding what I want to eat. I think I'll get a peanut butter chocolate candy bar with sprinkles on top."

"The candy you just described doesn't exist," I said.

Teeny furrowed her brow. "Well that's what I'm going to order."

I shook my head. "OK."

The energy inside the lobby was even more dreary than the energy out in the parking lot. The place was empty except for a pair of police officers who lingered near the water fountain. I didn't recognize either of them and assumed they were a couple of Mayor Linda Delgado's new hires. After the rash of murders that had happened in Pine Grove, Chief Sunshine Flanagan had demanded outside help to solve crimes. She said the force was spread too thin, but I was pretty sure she just wanted Miss May, Teeny, and me to stop showing her up.

Miss May approached the cops with a warm smile. "Excuse me. Is the *Phantom of the Opera* being performed here tonight?"

One of the police officers nodded. He was tall and skinny with a fresh face. Looked to be somewhere in his early 20's. "That's right. That crazy director is putting on the play even though his lead was murdered last night."

The second cop stepped forward. She was short and pudgy with a ponytail. "Pretty wacky, if you ask me. The guy seems out of his mind. Dresses like Mr. Rogers. Claims he spent a few years 'learning the habits of lions' in Africa."

"We're both new here," said the lanky cop. "Chief warned us this little town was filled with big time loonies. I didn't believe her until we hit the streets."

The lady cop murmured in agreement. "Same. I felt the same way. No way one small-town can have so many crazies, so many murders. Flanagan says there's a bunch of locals who think they're police officers, too. Creepy old ladies and some little karate sidekick who run around trying to solve the crimes."

Teeny scoffed. "They're not creepy. They're beautiful. And young. With very full lips."

The cops exchanged a look.

I nodded. "Yeah. The local amateur sleuths have the fullest lips in town. And none of them are 'sidekicks.' They're all equals." Miss May cleared her throat, but I was feeling defensive so I plowed ahead. "Also, the director of this play is a nice guy. He did a lot to help the lions in Africa. That's real. Plus, Mr. Rogers is cute. America loves him."

Miss May put one hand on Teeny's elbow and another on mine. "OK, girls. Let's leave these officers to their jobs. Nice to meet both of you."

The officers looked hesitant. The lanky officer narrowed his eyes. "Nice to meet you, too. Enjoy the show. I heard half the actors are playing it Southern, for some bizarre reason. So don't be surprised."

Teeny scoffed. "Our local actors are very talented. If they choose to go Southern for *Phantom of the Opera,* that is their artistic right."

"OK," said Miss May. "Let's go get some candy. Nice to meet you, officers."

"You already said that," the short officer said.

"Well I really mean it!" Miss May practically yelled as she guided us away. "What is wrong with you two? Finally there are cops in this town who don't know who we are and you act out like a couple of wackos."

"Told you," Teeny said. "Foot-in-mouth disease."

"I'm not going to let people talk about Germany that way," I said.

"We all know he's eccentric," Miss May said. "Eccentric

and odd and the stuff with the lions is weird. It's just weird, Chelsea. I know you know that. From an outside perspective, he is a highly unusual man."

"Of course I know that. But I don't want people to say that. Unless the people are me or you or Teeny."

Teeny nodded. "I'll say it. The kid is strange. Sometimes I wonder what you see in him. But he's sweet. I'll give him that. Sweet like a little puppy dog who follows you around everywhere you go."

I spotted the candy table across the room and nodded toward it. "Let's get some snacks for the show."

Miss May leaned toward me. "We're not here for the show, Chelsea. We're here to investigate."

I smiled. "Then snacks are even more important."

"Agreed," Teeny said, already halfway to the concessions stand.

The candy table had dozens of treats lined up on its surface. But no one was there to make the sale. Instead, a sign read: "Take what you want. Leave money."

Teeny turned down the sides of her mouth. "Wow. They couldn't even get that grumpy candy girl to come out to the show tonight."

"The lead was murdered yesterday," said Miss May. "Makes sense."

Teeny shrugged. "I like it this way. No one can judge me for what I buy." She dropped a $20 bill in the bucket and scooped half the candy bars on the table into her purse. "None of these have sprinkles but I suppose they'll have to do."

"Can I have one with peanut butter and caramel?" I peered into Teeny's purse. "Or something with white chocolate, if you have it."

Teeny pulled her purse close to her chest. "I wasn't planning to share."

I laughed. "You can't possibly eat all of those tonight."

Teeny exhaled. "Fine. Take what you want. But if I run out before intermission, you're buying me more."

"Once more," said Miss May. "We're not here to watch the play. We're here to conduct an investigation."

Teeny rolled her eyes. "Whatever."

Miss May grabbed one of Teeny's candy bars, unwrapped it, and took a bite. "Here's the plan.

I opened my candy bar too and took a bite. "Can the two of you try to go find Zambia? I want to look for Germany before the show."

"Sounds good." Teeny leaned forward. "But if you hear one of us scream, come save us."

I gave her a nervous smile. "I always do."

## 17

## HE LOVES ME NOT

*I* exited the lobby and headed down a long corridor in search of Germany. Being back in my high school had felt strange when I'd first returned to Pine Grove, but at that moment, I found the smells and sights of those familiar halls to be comforting. Reassuring, even. Like life was continuing, largely unchanged, in these hallways. Teenagers, with acne and insecurity and hopes and dreams, visited their lockers every day, rushed to class, skipped gym... there was something so nice about that idea.

I'd started at PGHS as a freshman, just a few months after my parents had died in a tragic car accident. I was introduced to my classmates as "that orphan girl." The vast majority of students had been kind to me but their kindness had made me uncomfortable. I had felt like a charity case in school and like no one had any interest in getting to know the real me.

Over the years I'd made a few good friends, and a few frenemies. I'd settled into my life in Pine Grove and found a sense of comfort in town, thanks to Miss May and her generosity and warmth. She was my mother's sister, so she'd also been grieving after my parents' death. But she'd put that grief aside and focused all of her attention on parenting me and helping me feel supported.

As I strolled down the hall, a row of class photos caught my eye. Each photo showed Pine Grove high school's graduating class, stretching back fifty or sixty years. I walked from picture to picture until I found my own graduating class.

I'd graduated with about 150 students. I scanned each row and remembered so many classmates by name. Then I found myself, right in the center of the picture. I barely recognized myself. There was my hair and there were my eyes. There was my small smile and there were my red cheeks. But who was that girl, sad and full of self-doubt and uncertainty about the future?

I thought about my parents. They never got to see me graduate from high school. They didn't know the girl in that picture at all. My eyes burned with the threat of tears, and I looked away from the picture.

It had been so hard adjusting to life after the death of my parents. And in that moment, I wondered if I ever truly had "adjusted." What does it mean to adjust to life after tragedy? How do you go on in the face of such a gaping, vital loss? I took a shaky breath, trying not to cry, but I felt a hiccuping sob shake my sides. *At least no one was around.*

"Chelsea."

I turned. Germany hurried toward me from the end of the hall. "Hey. Hey," he said. "You're OK."

Germany wrapped me in a hug. He pulled me close to his chest and I rested my head on his shoulder.

"I'm sorry," I said. "I'm crying on your director shirt."

"I don't care. Blow your nose in it if you need to."

I laughed through my tears. Germany was often deferent, long-winded, and quirky... but in that moment, he was just a solid presence. A figure of unwavering love. That felt good.

"What's going on?" Germany asked.

Germany was also an orphan, and I didn't really want to dump my emotions on him. So I tried to resist. "Oh, nothing. I just started looking at this photo and thinking about the past."

Germany nodded. "About how your parents never got to see you graduate from high school?" I looked up at him, surprised.

"Yes. How did you know that?"

"Because... we are the same in myriad ways, Chelsea Thomas. And for that reason, and so many others, I love you."

I stammered. I had not seen that coming.

*Did I love Germany?*

I hadn't thought about it. Maybe? But I didn't know what to say in that moment. I opened my mouth to speak, but then a shriek rang out from down the hall.

Germany whipped his head in the direction of the scream.

"What was that?" I asked. "Who's screaming?"

Another shriek exploded from down the hall. Germany looked back at me and gulped. "Zambia. It sounds like she's in trouble."

## 18

## SCREAM QUEEN

*G*ermany ran down the corridor. I jogged behind him, my heart racing. I wondered how much of the adrenaline rush I felt was from Germany's unexpected profession of love, and how much was from the threat of danger. A niggle of guilt wormed into my psyche — even though something terrible might have happened, I was relieved that Zambia's scream had bailed me out.

Germany and I burst into Zambia's dressing room in a panic. But what I saw was funnier and more terrifying than anything I would have anticipated.

Teeny and Miss May cowered against the back wall. Zambia stood in front of them, brandishing a hairdryer like a loaded gun.

"You two are terrible!" Zambia screamed. "Evil witches! I hate you both."

Teeny held up her hands in surrender. "OK, Zambia. You're right. We're horrible. Just, a couple of bad, bad witches. I admit it. Now please let us go."

Zambia shrieked, yet again. Germany took a careful step toward her. "Everything OK in here?"

Zambia turned and pointed the hairdryer at Germany. "Does everything look OK? Why aren't you protecting your actors? I'm trying to enter a calm headspace before my performance and these lunatics are bombarding me with questions. You are a bad director. Bad! You're supposed to protect me."

"Let's talk this through," said Germany. "Can you lower the hairdryer?"

"No. I will not lower the hairdryer. It is my only protection against these two, these two—"

"Witches?" Teeny supplied.

"Don't finish my thoughts, you witch!" Zambia yelled.

I cleared my throat and did my best to speak in a soft, calming voice. It came out like a squeaky, stressed-out mouse, but I tried. "Zambia. Hi, I'm Chelsea."

"I know who you are. You are with them."

"I just want to say... I know you lost your costar last night. So sorry that happened. It was a tragedy. Miss May, Teeny, and I want to help bring Adam justice. That's all."

"We tried to tell her that," said Teeny.

Zambia scoffed. "You think I'm a suspect, Little Woman! You and your stupid candy bars that you won't stop eating."

Teeny froze. Her hand was in her purse at that very moment, searching for a candy bar. She removed her hand from the purse and dropped a candy bar back inside. "I'm stressed. I eat candy when I'm stressed. Also, I eat candy when I'm happy and when I'm sad and when I'm angry."

"Everyone eats candy all the time," said Zambia. "Candy is delicious."

"I don't care for candy much, myself," said Germany. "Not unless it is homemade by Chelsea or her dear aunt."

Zambia shrieked once more. "Stop this inane chatter.

Why haven't you ejected these women from my dressing room?"

"You're right, Mrs. Mayor," said Germany. He turned to Teeny and Miss May. "Would you ladies be so kind as to vacate the dressing room?"

Teeny rolled her eyes. "That's what we were trying to do before she held us hostage with the hairdryer."

"I didn't hold anyone hostage." Zambia pulled at the hairdryer cord. "This thing isn't even plugged in."

Germany gestured toward the dressing room door. "Please. Let me have a moment alone with my actor."

Miss May nodded. "Of course. I'm sorry we disturbed you, Zambia."

Zambia seethed. "Get. Out."

Ten seconds later, Miss May, Teeny, and I were alone in the hall. Miss May paced back and forth. Teeny shook out her hands to try to relax. I watched them, dumbfounded.

"What happened in there?" I asked.

"Nothing." Teeny turned to me. "We asked a couple gentle questions about Zambia's relationship with Adam Smith. And she just lost it."

Miss May looked at Teeny over the brim of her glasses. "I asked a couple of gentle questions. You directly accused Zambia of murder. And adultery. And I also think you insulted her hair."

"I said I like the hair. It's perfect for her goofy face shape."

I put my head in my hands. "Oh my goodness. So what do you think? Is Zambia the lead suspect right now?"

Miss May shook her head. "It's hard to know. What you said was true, Chelsea... The poor woman just lost her costar. And if she and Adam were having an affair, she lost her lover as well."

"I hate the word lover," said Teeny. "Can we stop using that word? It creeps me out. Lover. Yuck."

"They were lovers, Teeny. That's the word."

"Maybe manstress? Or mister?" I suggested.

"Oh gross, even worse." Teeny wrinkled her nose.

I grabbed a candy bar from Teeny's purse, unwrapped it and took a bite. "Why did Germany call Zambia Mrs. Mayor, by the way? That was weird. Is that her character name or something?"

Teeny shook her head. "No. Zambia was mayor of Pine Grove for fifteen years. You didn't know that?"

"Chelsea was a little girl when Zambia was mayor. Little girls don't usually stay current on local politics."

"I guess that's true," said Teeny. "Local politics are the most boring thing in the universe unless you live in a town where people get murdered all the time."

"What if she had a political motive for the murder of Adam Smith?" I asked. "Our current mayor is a suspect in a lot of the cases we investigate. When people are in power it seems to put them in precarious situations more often than not."

Miss May shook her head. "Zambia was mayor so long ago. I don't think she killed for political reasons. Especially not if she and Adam were actually lovers."

"May. I'm not kidding." Teeny stuck out her tongue like she had just taken a sip of rancid milk. "I can't hear that word anymore."

I took another bite of candy bar. "So what should we do now?"

"Well... We need to find out more information from Zambia," said Miss May.

"So you want to watch the play? Try to talk again when

she gets out? Maybe apologize and have a real conversation?"

Miss May moved her head from side to side. "We could do that. But this play is three hours, right?"

I nodded. "Yeah. So?"

Miss May grinned. "That means Zambia's house is going to be empty until almost 11 PM."

Teeny smiled her biggest, most enthusiastic smiled. "Breaking and entering. My favorite."

## 19

## HUNKS OF JUNK

*W*hen we got back to Zambia's house, a junk removal van was parked in her driveway. The van was about fifteen feet long, and a logo on the side read "Junk Boys: We'll get rid of your junk." Not the most original slogan, but it got the point across. Below that, there was a phone number and address.

Miss May scratched her head as we walked up the driveway. "What the heck are the Junk Boys doing here? It's almost 9 o'clock."

"You know the Junk Boys?" I asked.

"Yeah, of course," Miss May said. "They're the boys you call when you need someone to move your junk."

I rolled my eyes.

"I bet you they were moving junk for Zambia." Teeny cupped her hands and looked in the back of the van. "These windows are tinted. I can't see anything."

"Wow. Nice detective work," I said.

"I'm doing my best, Chelsea." Teeny pointed around the back of the house. "There's a light on in the basement. Should we check it out?"

Miss May peered into the darkness. "I think I see a dumpster back there too. This is so weird."

I shrugged. "Looks to me like Zambia might be destroying evidence. Like maybe she paid the Junk Boys to come in the middle of the night. So no one would notice?"

Miss May chewed on her lower lip. "Maybe. But who hires a third-party to destroy criminal evidence? If Zambia had something to hide don't you think she would destroy the evidence herself?"

"Time is of the essence," I said. "And her ego is pretty big. She wanted to destroy the evidence but she wasn't willing to miss the second night of the play."

Teeny shook her head. "These actors are such narcissists. Look at me, look at me. Everything is about them. I had a cousin who was an actor once. She played a donkey in the school production of some play about donkeys."

"There aren't any plays about donkeys," said Miss May.

"Not after that production," said Teeny. "It was the one and only performance of, 'Donkeys are Funny, Hee-Haw, Hee-Haw.' It was terrible. You should consider yourself lucky if you've never seen a chorus of donkeys singing about falling in love."

Miss May laughed. "I'm going to go talk to the Junk Boys. See what they're up to. Are you two coming?"

I nodded. "Let's do it."

As we rounded the side of the house the Junk Boys dumpster came into full view. It was overflowing with furniture, papers and other odds and ends, presumably all from Zambia's home. Two men hurried in and out of the basement, grabbing stuff from inside and tossing it into the dumpster carelessly. Both of the men were big and bearded. They each wore large black headphones over their ears and worked silently and efficiently. *Like killers of junk.*

Miss May turned down the sides of her mouth. ""These guys are effective. And oblivious."

Teeny smiled. "And hunky."

I looked over at Teeny. "Hunky like...hot?"

Teeny shrugged. "Yeah. Why throw junk if you're not gonna get a good workout while doing it?" Teeny waved at one of the men to get his attention. He removed his headphones and walked over to us, eyes narrowed.

"Can I help you?" The man's voice was even bigger and burlier than he was.

Miss May stepped forward. "I think you can help us, thank you. We're here on behalf of Zambia, the homeowner? As she may have told you, she's performing in the play tonight so she couldn't be here."

"Oh, she told me," Junk Boy growled. "A few times."

"I'm sure," Miss May said. "Anyhow, she wanted us to come by and make sure you don't throw away her prized lamp collection."

The Junk Boy lit a cigarette. "Prized lamp collection? I haven't seen any prized lamp collection."

"I assure you she has one," said Miss May.

"Actually, she doesn't. I'm her brother, Al," the Junk Boy said. "My sister couldn't care less about lamps."

Miss May stammered. "Did I say lamps? Maybe I was confused. I'm just the messenger."

"Then what are these two?" Al asked, pointing at me and Teeny.

"Also messengers," Teeny said. "Don't shoot us!"

I laughed, a little too long and loud. "Yep, don't shoot the messengers. My uh, fellow messenger has the details a little off. Zambia didn't send us here for lamps. She sent us here for documents. Important documents. Life insurance papers. Home insurance papers. Stuff like that."

Al let out a puff of smoke. "Who did you say you were?"

Teeny stepped forward with a small wave. "Hi. I'm Teeny."

The man nodded. "I can see that."

"No. My name is Teeny. I'm also small. That's why they call me that. They call you Big Boy? Or Tall Guy?"

"They call me Al," Al said.

"Well you're very tall, Al," Teeny demurred.

Miss May looked over at Teeny. "You know who else is tall? Big Dan. Remember him?"

Al gave us a small smile. "Hey. You girls know Big Dan? Love that guy. He does great work."

"Yup. Wonderful mechanic. OK, so we're going to head inside and grab those papers. Then we'll be out of your hair." Miss May walked toward the basement door.

Al blocked her path. "I can't let you in there."

Miss May held up her hands. "I understand. You're in charge of the house while Zambia is gone. And you're her brother. You're protective. You don't know me. But I can assure you, I'm here to help. I'm a nice old lady, I promise."

Al scoffed. "Yeah, right. You think I don't know who you are? You three are those detectives. You think my sister's a killer."

Miss May let out a nervous laugh. "That's not true. Zambia's a brilliant actor and a kind woman and you seem like a wonderful brother."

The second man, Junk Boy Number Two, emerged from the basement. He crossed his arms. "What's going on out here?"

"Those local detective ladies are here. They said they're 'messengers,' but really they're here 'cuz they think Zambia killed Adam Smith."

Junk Boy Number Two stood tall and pulled out his phone. "I'll call the cops."

"No need for that," I said. "We'll get out of here. Just... If you see those insurance papers set them aside for Zambia, OK?"

Junk Boy Number Two did not put his phone away. "Get off this property. Now."

Teeny shook her head. "You two are so rude. I don't even think you're handsome anymore."

"Leave." Both men took a step toward us.

"OK," said Miss May. "You let Zambia know we came by. Tell her we saw you loading this dumpster. Tell her how suspicious that might seem, if viewed in a certain light."

The men laughed. Miss May shook her head and walked away. I followed. Teeny took one last look at the Junk Boys, then tagged along behind us.

"What now?" I asked.

Miss May exhaled. "Now we try to find a way inside that dumpster."

## 20

## DEEP SEA DUMPSTER DIVING

*W*e killed an hour eating potato chips in the gas station parking lot. Then we went to the Junk Boys building outside of town and parked along a chain-link fence. Miss May told me and Teeny we were headed there to scope the place out for a visit the next morning. But once the VW bus was in park, she turned to me with a mischievous glint in her eye and I knew she had other plans.

"I think one of us should sneak inside tonight and try to get a look at that dumpster."

I groaned. "You mean get a look <u>in</u> that dumpster?

"I guess," Miss May said.

"Ugh," I said. "You told me this was a stakeout. Not a deep-sea dive!"

Miss May shrugged. "I say a lot of things. My mind moves fast. I find a thread, I pull it. One duck, two duck, three duck, four."

"Don't confuse me with counting ducks," I said.

"I agree," said Teeny. "I was with you and then you started talking about ducks and now I'm completely lost."

Miss May removed her glasses and looked me in the eye. "Chelsea. Zambia is the number one suspect in this murder. She had her brother removed evidence from her home under the cover of his junk removal company. See that smokestack on the other side of this fence?"

Miss May pointed. I looked. Sure enough, there was a large smokestack about a hundred yards into the junk removal complex.

I gulped. "Yes?"

"That means there's an incinerator in that complex. Which means they have the capability to burn whatever they found in Zambia's home. Which means if one of us doesn't get in there tonight and investigate that dumpster... We might not have the evidence we need to solve this case."

Teeny bit her nails. "But we have a perfect record. We can't compromise our perfect record because we're too afraid to break into a junk removal place and dig around in a dumpster for a few minutes."

"I agree." Miss May looked back at me. "But neither Teeny nor I are young and spry enough to climb over that fence and hop into a dumpster."

"Hey. I'm young and spry." Teeny crossed her arms. "Maybe not spry. Or young. But I have a childlike energy. And people love the zest I bring to conversation. They say so all the time."

"What do you think, Chelsea?" Miss May unlocked the doors on the van. "You want to do some sleuthing?"

Did I want to climb a fence and sort through garbage in the middle of the night? *No.* Did I think I had a choice? *Definitely not.*

Miss May and Teeny had a bad habit of suggesting me for the tough jobs in our detective work. In our prior investigation they had convinced me to give a hairy man a massage to try to get information out of him.

"I'm still scarred by that time you two convinced me to give Lincoln the Elf a massage."

"That was a brave sacrifice," said Miss May. "Lincoln's back was disgusting. This is different."

I scoffed. "This is also disgusting. You're asking me to climb into a dumpster."

Miss May opened her door and stuck her foot up. "OK. I guess your little old aunt will go. I hope I don't dislocate a hip or get stuck at the top of the fence."

"Miss May—" I started

Teeny leaned forward. "Are you sure you want to do that, May? You're a weak old lady and there's no telling how hurt you might get attempting these acrobatics."

Miss May shrugged. "There's a killer on the loose. I'm willing to do whatever it takes for the greater good."

"Wow. You are a wonderful woman," said Teeny. "I admire and respect you for all you do for this community."

I sighed. "OK. I get it. I'll climb the fence and dig around in the dumpster."

Miss May turned back to me with big, puppy dog eyes. "Really? You'd do that just to protect my hips?"

"Your hips are fine," I said. I opened my door and stepped outside. "Just keep the van running." I closed the door and looked over at the junk removal building. It was two stories tall. Gray and foreboding. Surrounded by large green dumpsters.

I swallowed hard. Grabbed on to the chain-link fence and started climbing.

Climbing the fence was easier than I'd expected. When I'd first moved back to Pine Grove, I'd been out of shape and low on confidence. But since I'd started solving mysteries,

I'd been walking more, running more (mostly after criminals), and I'd brushed up on my karate. I hadn't realized it, but I was slowly getting back into fighting shape. Crime-fighting shape, that is.

Look, I'm not going to say I was graceful. I almost fell a few times. And by the time I got to the ground on the other side of the fence my underarms were drenched in sweat. And I was also sweating behind my knees. But I made it without so much as a scrape. So when my feet hit the pavement, I felt proud and confident.

When I turned and looked at all the dumpsters, my heart sank. There had to be at least twenty. There was no way I would have time to look through every single one in order to determine which contained Zambia's belongings.

I surveyed the area. Half of the dumpsters had been stacked deep against the building. They were blocked by a second stack of dumpsters so none of those could belong to Zambia. But any one of the remaining ten could possibly hold Zambia's things.

I crept toward the dumpsters with caution. How would I be able to figure out which dumpster belong to Zambia? I stopped walking, closed my eyes and thought.

Images of the burly men darted through my mind. I saw them tossing furniture into the dumpster. And I remembered seeing them dump box after box of paper into the dumpster as well. Then I remembered seeing one of the Junk Boys toss an entire mini refrigerator filled with food into the dumpster.

I remembered thinking, "What a waste of perfectly good food." And that gave me an idea... I scanned the dumpsters, looking carefully. Then I saw what I was looking for...

A raccoon.

I knew from my time at the orchard that raccoons were

like heat-seeking missiles for food, no matter how disgusting that food might be. I reasoned that the raccoon was drawn to the food from Zambia's miniature fridge and plodded toward that dumpster.

I approached and saw I was right — I recognized the mini fridge and also the hideous sofa from Zambia's house. *One problem...* I groaned. How did I let Teeny and Miss May talk me into this stuff? And how was I going to scare off those raccoons so I could jump into the dumpster?

I looked around the junkyard, searching for something I could clang together to startle the foraging animal. I spotted an old, iron pipe sticking out of the adjacent dumpster. I climbed on the edge of the dumpster, grabbed the pipe and jumped back down.

I turned back to Zambia's dumpster. I could hear multiple raccoons now, undoubtedly all feasting on the contents of that mini fridge. I took a deep breath, pulled back the pipe and banged it against the side of the dumpster.

Bang. Bang. Bang-bang-bang.

The raccoons darted out of the dumpster with stunning alacrity, leapt onto the chain-link fence and disappeared into the night.

I put my hand to my chest and laughed. So much action-packed adventure, and I hadn't even climbed inside the dumpster yet.

One minute later, I was knee-deep in Zambia's trash. I stayed away from the miniature fridge, because I doubted any of the evidence I needed would be edible.

I grabbed a garbage bag and ripped it open. Inside: dozens of stuffed polar bears, each one identical to the other. I dug into the bag. The polar bears were soft and cuddly. I picked one up and squeezed it. So cute.

One of the polar bears still had a tag attached to the ear. I opened the tag and read the note inside.

"To Z: all my love. You are the polar bear of my heart — fierce, ferocious, yet cuddly. Love, A."

If Z stood for Zambia, and A stood for Adam...this bear confirmed that Zambia was having an affair with Adam. And it confirmed that Adam truly loved her. Either that, or he had the hook-up for very cheap stuffed polar bears.

The polar bears weren't evidence of murder but they were a good start. But if Adam loved Zambia enough to shower her in adorable little gifts, why wouldn't he leave his wife?

My mind raced as I continue to dig through the dumpster. I found several more love notes written from Adam that were addressed to Zambia. Then I spotted what appeared to be another giant polar bear on the far side of the dumpster and I tried to make my way toward it.

I took an uneasy step into the junk and nearly toppled over. The piles beneath me were uneven and covered with debris. I took another step toward the giant polar bear and stumbled yet again. That time, my foot caught on an old typewriter and I fell face first into the junk.

I landed hard on my elbow and yelped. I'm not sure if you've ever taken a hard fall inside a dirty dumpster... But I wouldn't recommend it. *Gross. And painful.*

I tried to climb to my feet, then a voice called out from above me.

"Chelsea. Are you OK?"

I looked up and was blinded by a bright flashlight. I shielded my eyes and saw the man behind the light. It was Detective Wayne Hudson. And once again, he did not look happy.

## 21

## WHERE THERE'S A WILL, THERE'S A WAYNE

"*I* don't want to arrest you. I don't." Wayne handed me a cup of coffee and sat beside me on the curb. Even though Wayne and I weren't a romantic item, I still felt self-conscious about being covered in trash and smelling like an old mini fridge. I tried to brush some debris off my shirt.

"Because... I looked so cute in the dumpster?"

"No. The paperwork gives me a headache. It's late on a Saturday. It's too much."

I sipped my coffee. "Does that mean I'm free to go?"

We were sitting outside the junk removal building. I could see Miss May's van idling on the other side of the fence. In my mind, I jumped to my feet, scaled the fence, and hopped into the car in five seconds flat. But in reality, my tush stayed planted on the curb, right beside Wayne.

"You're not free to go quite yet." Wayne slurped from his cup of coffee. "Because we're still talking."

"Are we talking as a police officer and a potential criminal? Or are we talking as friends?"

Wayne looked at me out of the side of his eyes. "You tell me. Are we friends?"

I looked down. I was definitely dating Germany. Wayne knew that. But Wayne hadn't really moved on. Part of that was my fault. The two of us had a good vibe a lot of the time, and I liked it. Wayne was handsome, and our verbal sparring too easily transformed to flirting.

"You did look cute in the dumpster, by the way," Wayne said.

I gave Wayne a small smile. "Thanks."

"That's saying a lot."

I shrugged. "There were a few raccoons in there when I arrived. They looked cute. Pretty effortlessly."

"So are you saying you're...like a raccoon?"

I laughed. "I guess. Small. Scrappy. Resourceful."

We sat in silence for a few seconds. I glanced back at Miss May's van. So close yet not close enough.

Unless... I just made the decision to leave.

I stood up. "OK. I'm going to leave now."

Wayne stood beside me. "Hang on."

I shook my head. "I can't. It's late. Miss May and Teeny are waiting."

"You are breaking the law here."

"I know. If you need to arrest me, then arrest me. But we both know we're on the same side. Don't forget, Miss May, Teeny, and I have solved all the recent murders in Pine Grove. In case you're keeping score, that's cute sleuths: Ten. Police: Zero."

Wayne scoffed. "That's not fair. You needed my help in several of those cases."

"I don't need your help right now. All I need is for you to let me leave." I felt a familiar flush of annoyance at Wayne.

Like he was trying to undermine me or suggest that I couldn't do things on my own. Part of that was probably projection, but part of that was real — and it was why I had shied away from a romantic partnership with Detective Hudson.

"I'm not detaining you, Chelsea. I thought we were talking. I gave you coffee."

"So you thought now would be a good time to what, catch up? You caught me in Zambia's dumpster, Wayne. I've been scared of you this entire conversation. Scared that you're going to arrest me."

"Why would you—"

"Because you kept implying it. You're using your power as a police officer to intimidate me into talking to you." Wayne and I were both strong-willed — it had taken me a while to find my voice, sure. But now that I had it, I wasn't backing down from this conversation.

Wayne looked away. "I didn't think of it like that. I'm sorry. I really thought this was just a conversation between two equals. I want you to know that."

I nodded. "OK."

"I would never arrest you, Chelsea. I thought...I thought that was clear. I took it for granted that you knew that. You're right. The three of you are good for this town. You catch killers. I get that, but Chief Flanagan doesn't. And if someone else showed up at the scene tonight... You would have gone to jail. And you would have had to serve time."

"I know." I did know, but hearing Wayne say it such frank terms was still alarming.

"So I guess that's what I was trying to work around to on the curb here. I wasn't holding you hostage. I was trying to find a way to say that you need to be more careful. Because I don't want to see you in jail. And if that happens, and it's because you were snooping around illegally? I'm not going to be able to help you."

I looked up. Wayne's eyes were tired and sad. He furrowed his brow. "I don't want to see anything bad happen to you. Because you're...my friend."

I felt a wave of regret. Although I knew I had been right to speak my mind with Wayne, he had a good point. Breaking into the junk removal place that night was reckless. And Miss May, Teeny, and I needed to be more cautious. Fly lower under the radar.

"You're right," I said. "Those are all good points."

Wayne nodded. "Tell the girls I said hi?"

"OK. I will."

"You think the three of you are close to finding the killer?"

I shrugged. "I hope so."

Wayne finished coffee and crumpled the cup. "Me too. Because we've got no idea."

## 22

# ALL'S FAIR IN LOVE AND MURDER

*T*eeny and Miss May peppered me with questions as we drove home. First and foremost, they wanted to know what had happened with Wayne. Surprising, I know, considering we were in the midst of a murder investigation. But those two loved to gossip about their favorite topic which was, well, love.

Miss May smirked at me in the rearview mirror as she drove. "So did he touch your hand? Did he smell like cinnamon and vanilla?"

Teeny giggled. "Did he tell you you looked beautiful in that dumpster? And did he say that no amount of trash could dim your wondrous, bright light?"

Miss May laughed and smacked the steering wheel. "I can't believe he found you in the trash."

"It's not that funny," I said. "The dumpster was pretty clean, as far as garbage goes. Mostly furniture, one mini fridge, some stuffed animals, a few love notes, stuff like that. But you're not interested in the contents of the dumpster. You'd rather I discuss whether or not Wayne smelled like cinnamon. He didn't. I didn't smell him. My nose was clogged with trash smells."

Miss May looked back at me. "Did you say love notes?"

Over the next few minutes, I debriefed Teeny and Miss May on everything I had come across in the dumpster. I told them the truth. I had not found any truly definitive evidence that Zambia and Adam were having an affair. But all the love notes were from A to Z and that seemed to suggest the likelihood of an illicit romance.

I let out a long, deep sigh as I concluded. "Would've been nice to have more time in the dumpster, actually. There was so much I didn't have a chance to search through. If Zambia is guilty... The evidence must be there."

Miss May turned up Whitehill Road and the VW bus chugged toward the top of the hill. "That's the problem with breaking and entering. You never know how much time you're going to have."

"I know," I said. "Wayne said I was lucky that he was the one who showed up on the scene. And he was right. If that had been Flanagan who caught me dumpster diving... Or even Hercules..."

Teeny nodded. "Oh yeah. If Flanagan discovered you covered in all that putrid, stinky garbage? She wouldn't think you looked cute. She would have pulled you out by your tangled hair, thrown you to the ground, and slapped handcuffs on your wrists, all in ten seconds flat."

"You think my hair is tangled?" I asked.

"Very," Teeny said.

"I don't know that Flanagan would be that extreme." Miss May pulled into our driveway.

Teeny shrugged. "I left out the part in my imagination where Flanagan pistol-whipped all three of us."

"Can we change the subject?" I would have rather

discussed anything else, including Teeny's low opinion of my grooming.

"Sure." Miss May pointed toward the farmhouse. "Let's talk about that."

I looked out the window. Zambia was sitting on the front steps of the farmhouse. She stood as we approached and crossed her arms. Her eyes were hard and set. Her fists were clenched. I suddenly felt guilty for rifling through Zambia's trash earlier in the night. Although we needed to see what was in that dumpster, coming face to face with the owner of those belongings, I felt like I had invaded her privacy. My palms turned into a couple of clams as Miss May parked and turned back to me.

"I hope you're ready for a fight."

I swallowed. "Always." Miss May looked skeptical. "What? I am! I'm ready." I mumbled under my breath, "Sort of."

Miss May gave Zambia a warm smile as we approached. "Zambia. I'm so glad you're here. Teeny and I have been talking all night. We shouldn't have intruded on you while you were preparing for the play this evening. That was wrong and I'm sorry."

Zambia ran her tongue along her teeth, annoyed. "How dare you apologize to me? You are not sorry. The only thing you regret is not finding out more information from me when you were attacking me in that dressing room."

Teeny stepped forward. "That's not true. I also ate way too much candy tonight. Now I'm a little dizzy. So I regret that."

Once again, I tried to change the subject. "How did the performance go tonight?"

Zambia turned on me. "No one died, if that's what you're asking."

"I wasn't asking that. Although I'll admit I'm glad there were no fatalities during the show. Did you have fun? Did people show up to watch?"

Zambia shook her head. "The place was empty. All I could hear was the echo of my own voice. And the sound of Germany sighing backstage."

Zambia looked off into the distance for a long moment. She had big circles under her eyes and she bit her lower lip. Her arms were wrapped around her torso like she was giving herself a hug. It looked like she might have been fighting off tears. My thoughts darted back to all those stuffed polar bears.

Teeny tiptoed around Zambia and headed toward the farmhouse. "Good night, then. Wonderful to see you, as always. I'm sure you broke a leg out there. But I'm glad no one died. Hope we can catch you in the next performance. You're a true star."

Zambia spun around and glared at Teeny. "Don't you take one step closer to that house."

I heard Steve barking from inside. KP had fed him and taken him out. But the poor guy was probably on edge because a possible murderer had been sitting on the steps outside his house.

Teeny paused, mid-step. She let out a nervous giggle. "Yes, ma'am."

Miss May cleared her throat and looked right at Zambia. "What can we help you with?"

"You can stop right there and listen to what I have to say," Zambia snarled.

Miss May and I exchanged a worried glance. I placed my hand in the pocket of my sweatshirt.My body tensed, ready for a fight.

Miss May turned up her hand in a gesture of openness. "Start talking."

Zambia began to pace back and forth. "First of all, I am deeply hurt that any of you think I could have killed Adam. He was such a sweet man. Gentle and tender."

"We know that," said Teeny. "But you are kind of scary."

*Fierce, ferocious, yet cuddly*, I thought, remembering Adam's note.

Zambia exhaled through her nose. "I am not scary. I'm a woman of the theater. Yes, I am serious. But I have deep love in my heart. Most of it is for Adam Smith."

Miss May nodded. "We never said we suspected you."

Zambia laughed, a little too long and a little too hard. "Second: I cannot believe you snuck into my brother's facility and dug around in my trash."

"We did not do that," said Teeny. "That sounds disgusting."

"We didn't even know your brother owned Junk Boys," I said. "We spent the last three hours doing exercise...in a field."

"Yep," said Teeny. "Jumping jacks, mostly. Although I think that's kind of a sexist name for an exercise. Why can't they be jumping jills?"

Zambia sighed. "I don't have time for these babbling lies. I know you were digging through my trash. So I suppose you're now aware of the depth of my relationship with Adam."

My number one goal as a detective? *Get better at excuses.* "Yes," I said. "I was in your trash. I saw the notes."

"It seems like you had a wonderful connection," said Miss May. "I'm sorry we invaded your privacy. It's just... When we see someone clearing out their house the night after a murder... It does raise our suspicions."

"I'm not destroying the evidence of a murder," said Zambia. "I'm destroying the evidence that Adam and I were ever romantically intertwined. He was a married man. I don't want to cast any aspersions on him now that he's dead. No one needs to know about our relationship. Adam shouldn't be remembered as a cheater. He was an honorable man."

Miss May scratched her head. "Did Adam's wife know about the two of you?"

Zambia shook her head. "Dorothy didn't know anything. She suspected, but she didn't know. That's what I'm trying to say. Please don't tell anyone what you found in that dumpster."

"We won't," said Miss May. "But Dorothy seemed so upset when you and Adam kissed on stage. Almost like... she knew every detail of your relationship with Adam."

"When Dorothy stormed out... That was a reaction to our clear chemistry on stage. I have no idea how strongly she'd react if she knew the whole truth."

Miss May, Teeny, and I said goodbye to Zambia and headed inside. When Miss May locked the front door behind us and turned back to me, I saw that her face was white and scared.

"What's the matter?" I asked.

Miss May exhaled. "We've got a lot of work to do."

## 23

## CUCKOO FOR COCOA

*D*elicious hot chocolate might be one of my favorite things in the world. I won't bore you with the details of my long history with hot chocolate, I'll just say this: As far as I'm concerned, a good cup of cocoa always comes down to the the person who's making it. And the ingredients. And the time. *Oh, who am I kidding? I'm about to bore you with the details.*

When I was a kid, I'd loved the Swiss Miss stuff. Those little blue packages and hard tiny marshmallows delighted me every Christmas morning. And lots of other mornings throughout the winter. I used to like nothing more than coming inside from playing in the snow and seeing those packages out on the counter. Then, my parents and I would curl up by the fire and sip hot cocoa while we laughed, sang songs, or played a board game.

As I got older, my tastes in hot chocolate got a bit more sophisticated. In my adulthood, I found myself drawn toward the hot cocoa that started with fine, dark chocolate shavings from fancy chocolate shops. Snobby, I know. But that stuff gets so silky smooth and rich in your favorite mug... It's one of the best tastes on earth. Blame Miss May — her hot cocoa is the best.

I also started to prefer fresh milk from a local farm. Or almond milk or oat milk from the store. Before you knock it, you should try it. Sometimes, a hint of nutty or oaty flavor does a lot to elevate the flavors of the chocolate. A little whipped cream on top — heaven in a cup.

Take a moment and imagine it with me. You curl your fingers around the handle of your favorite coffee mug. The whipped cream has begun to melt into the rich, chocolate liquid. You bring the mug to your lips, and you feel the cool whipped cream on your upper lip. You tilt the mug back and your mouth fills with velvety, smooth chocolate. It stays in your mouth a moment, then you swallow and feel the hot chocolate snaking its way down into your stomach and warming your entire body. Any and all your worries and troubles disappear, if only for a moment.

*Yeah. I love hot chocolate.*

So the morning after Miss May, Teeny, and I spoke to Zambia outside the farmhouse, I was thrilled when Miss May suggested we head into town and go to the *Brown Cow* for hot chocolate. Brian, the relaxed SoCal transplant who owned our local coffee shop, made the best hot chocolate in Pine Grove-slash-the-universe. I pulled on the clothes I had been wearing the night before, let Steve out to do his morning business, then jumped into the VW bus to join Miss May for a cup.

Small-town conversation can be just as cozy as hot chocolate. So I hung out near the counter and chatted with Brian as he made my drink.

"What's new in here lately?"

Brian gave me his signature, California surfer smirk.

Slow and steady with just a hint of mischief. "Nothing new. Nothing old. Taking it one day at a time."

I nodded. "Deep."

Brian laughed. "Yeah. I've been listening to a podcast about meditation. Trying to implement the practices in my daily life. You used to be pretty into that stuff, right?"

I laughed. "Yeah. When I first moved to town I had a pretty steady practice. Back when I was living in the city, I think I needed it to stay calm and grounded. But once I moved back here... I started to feel naturally more present in each moment. I didn't have to center myself, it just happened. But I still love meditation, don't get me wrong."

Brian looked up and smiled at me. "I'm glad you like it here. It's been awesome having you around, even with all the murders. I guess especially with all the murders, since you keep solving 'em."

I smiled. "I'm glad I'm back. It's been awesome having a local coffee shop that isn't filled with strangers in a hurry."

"Tell me about it," said Brian. "Those city coffee shops are ridiculous. Super small. Coffee costs a fortune. The people who work there are always rude."

"And they're always crowded," I said.

Brian pointed at me. "Exactly. And not crowded in a good way. Crowded like you can barely wiggle your way to the counter to order a latte."

I nodded. "Yep."

Brian gestured at a middle-aged man who was sitting over by the window. The man was wearing all black and had a bushy, brown mustache.

"Got a classic city snob in here this morning." Brian spoke in a hushed tone. "I think he's some kind of important newspaper guy. Took like fifteen minutes to order, asked a million stupid questions, and didn't leave a tip."

The snobby man stood and gathered his things. He took his time as he finished his coffee then threw the cup in the trash. Then he smoothed out his shirt, pulled up his sleeves, zipped his jacket all the way up to his turtleneck, and headed out.

"Seems like a particular guy," I said.

"Particular and demanding. I had to remake his drink three times."

I gave Brian a small laugh. "I wonder what he's doing in Pine Grove."

"I think he was writing an article about Adam Smith. I assumed the guy was a theater critic or something like that. Not sure, though."

Liz, our very own local reporter extraordinaire, approached from nearby. "You two don't know who that guy was?"

Brian and I shrugged at the same time in the exact same manner. Liz shook her head. "That's Edward Frame. The most famous entertainment reporter in the history of time. He's been the entertainment editor of a very prestigious New York City newspaper for my whole life. Frame's a legend. I introduced myself and texted him my resume. He seemed impressed by my credentials."

Brian nodded. "I knew he was a theater guy."

"You think Edward is in town because there's some sort of story with Adam?" I asked.

Liz nodded. "Definitely. Maybe they're doing a retrospective of Adam's career on Broadway. Maybe Frame and Adam were friends back in the day." Liz's eyes widened. "Maybe Adam was at the heart of some kind of long-running scandal and Edward is looking for a scoop."

"Miss May and I should talk to that guy," I said.

"You better vamoose." Liz pointed out the window,

where I could see Edward climbing into a little sedan. "He's about to leave."

Teeny burst into the coffee shop, just at that moment. "Famous reporter Edward Frame's outside and he's about to leave!"

"We know," I said. "Let's go."

## 24

## TWO SCOOPS OF MURDER

"We're taking my convertible." Teeny darted to her car and climbed in. Miss May and I followed.

"Please drive safe." Miss May buckled up. "He's not that far ahead of us. We don't need to drive too fast."

"Hey, this is my chase scene, May. You just sit there and be a good copilot."

I leaned forward. "I'd like to cast a second vote for driving at a normal speed."

"This ain't a democracy, Chels! Besides, there could be lives on the line." Teeny jammed her keys into the ignition, yanked the car into drive, and peeled out of her parking spot. "Here we go, baby! Time to see what this pink rocket can do."

Teeny slammed on the brakes to stop at a crosswalk. Petunia and Ethel were crossing with their walkers. They were not moving fast. Teeny gave them the right-of-way, but I could tell she was itching to speed around them. "Good morning, ladies. Take your time. We're not in a high-speed chase or anything."

Petunia glared at Teeny. "Still driving this midlife crisis machine, Teeny? You look like an Over-The-Hill Barbie!"

"Hey, at least I look like Barbie at some age!" Teeny countered. Petunia made an obscene gesture. Teeny smiled and offered a thumbs-up in return. "Love you, too, Petunia."

Petunia and Ethel reached the other side of the road and Teeny pressed the pedal to the metal once more. Thirty seconds later, we were leaving Pine Grove and speeding up an on-ramp toward the highway.

"Where are you going, Teeny?" Miss May asked.

"You said he's a theater critic, right? From the city? I'm headed to the city."

"It's going to be hard to find one guy in New York City," I said. "We need to catch up to him."

"You should have taken the back roads," Miss May grumbled. "This is going to be longer."

"Disagree, May. Thank you for your input."

I pointed up ahead of us. "Isn't that his car?"

Teeny's eyes widened. "Told you I was good."

Teeny laid on her horn. Beep. Beep. I could see Edward's face in his rearview mirror. He seemed startled and confused. He craned his neck back and held his hand up as if to say, "What's wrong?"

Teeny stuck her head outside. "Pull over. This is important. We need to talk."

The man's eyes widened. He did not appear comforted by the sight of a tiny blonde lady driving a tiny pink convertible screaming out the open top. He sped up.

"Great job, Teeny. He's getting away." Miss May stuck her head out her window. "We don't want to hurt you. All we need is five minutes."

I leaned forward from the back seat. "There's no way

that guy can hear you. We're driving 70 mph on the highway. And he's thirty feet in front of us."

Miss May turned back to me. "Will you mind your own business?"

"Um, this is definitely my business," I said. "It's not like I'm working on something besides this car chase in the backseat."

Teeny glared at me in the rearview mirror. "Then mind someone else's business. Spend some time thinking about peace in the Middle East. Something like that."

Miss May turned to Teeny. "Is there a toll coming up?"

Teeny shrugged. "Yeah. I have EZ Pass."

"But I'm sure Frame does too. We need to cut him off before he speeds through the toll."

"If we take the back roads we can skip the toll, then maybe we can cut him off of the bridge." I pulled up a map on my phone. "It'll be close but it's possible."

Teeny shook her head. "Put that phone away. I have a better idea." Edward slowed his car as he approached the toll booth. Teeny sped up. She placed her hands at ten and two on the wheel and held on tight.

Miss May looked at Teeny out of the corner of her eyes. "Teeny. What are you doing? We're in the cash only lane."

Teeny took a breath. "Hang on tight, ladies."

Teeny blasted through the gate in the cash lane of the toll booth, swung her car around, and blocked the EZ pass lane, just in time to stop Edward from getting away. The toll-booth worker, a teenage boy wearing a khaki uniform with wide, garish stripes, hurried over toward us.

"Hey," the teenage boy said. "What are you doing? You just destroyed my gate."

"Harry Mendelson. Go back into your tollbooth," Teeny

said. "I know your mother. Everything is fine. This is important adult stuff."

The teenage boy's voice cracked. "You know my mom?"

"That's right. Don't believe me? Get in there and call your mother. Tell her Teeny says hello. She'll tell you there's nothing to worry about. I'm going to cover the cost of the gate. Just leave me alone for five minutes."

Harry took a couple steps back toward his booth. "OK. Cool car."

Teeny nodded. "Thank you. I know."

Edward Frame climbed out of his sedan with his hands held up. "Hey. You're blocking my path. And you nudged my front bumper."

Teeny waved Edward off. "Nudge, smudge. There's not a mark on either of our cars."

Miss May stepped forward. "Still, if we did nudge you," she said, "we're so sorry. The three of us got caught up chatting, we blew through the gate, we made a wild turn. We're completely at fault. Let's exchange insurance information."

Miss May looked over at Teeny. Teeny nodded. "Yes. We should exchange... information."

"This is your fault." The man pulled his insurance card out of his wallet and handed it to us. Teeny did the same.

"You're absolutely right," she said. "I can be a very distracted driver. Here's my license... Don't look at the photo, I was having a bad hair day. Can I get yours, too? Take a photo just in case?"

The man chuckled. "I think this is a nice photo." He handed his license to Teeny. "I was having a no hair day."

Teeny laughed and took a photo of the man's ID. I watched as she zoomed in and took a photo of just the man's address. I smirked. She looked at me and smirked. And suddenly I knew where we were headed next.

## 25

## WINE AND TEASE

"*I* was about to ask him about Adam Smith. You stopped me dead in my tracks." Teeny put the keys in the ignition and put the car in drive. "I'm a sleuth too, you know."

"I respect that," said Miss May. "But you had just run into the guy. He was already on edge. That's not the best time to get information from a suspect."

"This guy is a suspect now?" I asked.

Miss May shook her head. "No. He's not a suspect. But you know what I mean. If you need information from someone you need to butter them up. Bring them a pie. Put a smile on their face. Not cut them off when they're going through a toll."

"You have your methods, I have mine," Teeny said.

I buckled my seatbelt. "So what do we do now? Teeny, I saw you took a picture of his address. But we don't need to break into his apartment. We need to talk to him."

"I have an idea," said Miss May. "Take that exit for New York City."

An hour and a half later, we were double-parked outside

Edward's apartment in Manhattan's West Village. Several prior investigations had taken us into New York City. Each visit to the city had been exciting and mysterious. I assumed that this visit would be the same.

At that moment, however, our evening didn't seem too promising. There were no lights on in Edward's apartment. Plus, the front door was locked and we hadn't managed to sneak inside the building.

"I don't understand this plan." Teeny reached into her purse, opened a bag of pretzels, and popped one in her mouth. "If we're not going to sneak into his apartment to see what we can learn, why are we here?"

"Because we need to talk to Edward," Miss May said, for the millionth time. "As of now, he doesn't know us at all. He thinks we're three kooky ladies who damaged his car on the highway. But I don't think he had a negative experience with us. We were gracious, we seemed willing to pay for the damage, I think he liked us."

I shrugged. "How does that help?"

"If we stake this place out, we can catch Edward on the sidewalk when he's coming or going. We can pretend it's a chance encounter. Maybe take him to dinner or something. Buy him a few glasses of wine. See what we can learn."

"That's going to be tough to pull off," I said. "He seems like a busy guy. And the kind of guy who maybe doesn't believe in coincidence."

Miss May shrugged. "Can't be harder than solving a murder."

Teeny stuck her head out the window and craned her neck up to get a better look at the top floor apartment where we assumed Edward lived. "He's got a nice place up there. Plush carpets. Framed photos of himself with famous Broadway actors. The giant TV screen where he probably gathers with friends to watch the Oscars and the Tony's. And he's got one of those refrigerators that makes water and coffee and seltzer and dispenses fresh draft beer."

"I don't think they make refrigerators that dispense beer," I said.

Teeny pulled her head back into the car. "Agree to disagree."

A man crouched down beside Teeny's open window. "My refrigerator is much more normal than that."

The three of us shrieked and practically jumped out of our seats.

I pressed my hand to my chest and leaned forward to get a better look at the man in the window. Sure enough, it was Edward Frame, the theater critic. He gave me a small smile.

"I had a feeling that accident by the tollbooth was more than an accident." He looked at me. "You're right, I don't believe in coincidence. How can I help you ladies?"

A few moments later, Edward led us into his top floor apartment. It was decorated in a posh, modern style. A spotless white leather couch faced a double-sided fireplace. The kitchen was sleek, with clean lines and beautiful marble countertops and those cabinets that closed softly and never slammed.

Miss May, Teeny, and I spent a few minutes praising the elegant apartment. Then Edward poured us each a glass of red wine and gestured for us to take a seat on the couch. My interior design brain freaked out at the thought of red wine on a white couch, but I kept my cool.

"Please," Edward said. "Tell me why you're really here. Tell me why you crashed into my car on the highway this afternoon."

"Oh, I barely nudged it!" Teeny protested.

"Sorry again," said Miss May. "We'll tell you everything.

I'm impressed you detected our ulterior motives with such ease."

Edward shrugged and settled back into the couch. "I'm a reporter. Sure, maybe I cover entertainment. But still... I make my living sussing out the truth."

Miss May nodded. "As do we."

"Well, not really our living," I said. "We sell apples for a living. Whatever. Sorry I interrupted. Please, continue."

Miss May shot me a look, then gestured to herself, me, and Teeny. "We're small-town detectives. Amateur sleuths. Trying to solve the murder of Adam Smith. I suspect Adam's death is what brought you to Pine Grove this afternoon?"

Edward gave Miss May a small nod. "I knew Adam for decades. His death was unexpected. But I take small solace knowing he died during a performance. He was never more comfortable than when he was on stage."

Edward spoke with a careful precision, like he considered every word before he said it. That manner of speaking was not familiar to me. I blurted out every thought that came into my mind and had a problem with babbling. I bit my fingernails to keep from saying anything stupid.

Edward seemed nice enough. But working murder after murder, I'd learned to suspect everyone. I wondered, *Was Edward hiding something? Could he have killed Adam?*

Teeny sipped her wine. "But you wouldn't have come all the way up to our little town just to write an obituary for Adam. There must be something more to the story."

Frame raised his eyebrows. "There's always something more to the story."

"Well what is it? Tell us already." Teeny threw up her hands.

I laughed. Teeny had never been one for small talk in urgent situations.

Edward laughed right along with me. "I like you. You say what's on your mind."

"Sometimes I put my foot too close to my mouth, that's for sure," Teeny said. "Wine doesn't help. Especially when I'm thirsty and it's good wine."

Edward sipped from his own glass. "I'm glad you like it."

"I still want to know what information you've got," said Teeny. "Enough beating around the bushes!"

Miss May leaned forward a bit. "Teeny. It's OK if Edward doesn't want to share his inside scoop. He's a reporter. He makes his trade learning the truth and learning how to keep a secret."

"Well said," Edward said. "I also make my living by assessing who I can trust and who I can't. I can tell... The three of you are trustworthy. You want to find justice for Adam."

Miss May exhaled. "That's all we're after."

Edward stood and crossed back to the kitchen to pour himself another glass of wine. "Then let me tell you all about Adam Smith's enemies on Broadway."

"Enemies... Plural?" Miss May stood. "How many people hated this guy?"

"Plenty. But I can only think of one person who wanted him dead."

## 26

# THE CAT'S MEOW

*O*ver the course of the next hour, Edward Frame regaled us (in grand, dramatic fashion) with the story of Adam Smith's arch-rival — one of the "unnamed cats" from the hit Broadway musical *CATS*.

At first, neither Miss May nor Teeny believed Edward. I didn't either, for that matter. Why would an actor from *CATS* want Adam Smith dead?

"Why would an actor from *CATS* want Adam Smith dead?" I asked out loud.

Edward, obviously objecting to my skepticism, launched into a long story about stolen parts and roommates and the competitive nature of actors trying to make a living on Broadway. Based on his tone, Edward thought every second of his story was riveting, but I almost fell asleep at least three times. Finally, at the end of his long-winded story, he got to the point...

Adam Smith's Broadway nemesis was a big, bald man named Ace. Turns out, Ace was still performing every night as "unnamed cat" in *CATS*. That was our next big lead, and even though we were two bottles of wine deep into conversation with Mr. Frame, we all politely excused ourselves and bolted out of there.

We arrived at the Neil Simon theater in Midtown Manhattan at around 9 PM. The street exploded with energy. A caricature artist drew a picture of a happy little girl. Tipsy 20-something girls stumbled out of a sports bar. A homeless man slumped against the wall, shaking his cup for change.

Dozens of well-dressed people stood outside the theater lobby, eating candy and chatting.

"It must be intermission," I said. "If we find the actors entrance we can probably catch Ace after the play. I think they have to enter and exit through a special door."

"So you want to just stand out here for another two hours waiting?" Teeny shook her head. "No way. We're going to second-act this thing."

I furrowed my brow. "What is second-acting?"

Miss May laughed. "One of the oldest tricks in the book."

"Let me tell it. And don't call my tricks old!" Teeny looked both ways to make sure no one was listening. "When you second-act a play, that means you wait outside at intermission, then when the crowds hurry back in for the second act... You join the masses and hurry in along with them. I used to do it all the time back in my 20's."

Miss May chuckled. "So just a few years ago then?"

"That's right," said Teeny.

Inside the lobby, the lights flickered. Teeny's eyes widened. "That's the signal. You girls ready?"

I thought about objecting, but I knew it was pointless. Before I could even open my mouth to agree, Teeny grabbed me and Miss May by our elbows and led us into the theater.

My clam-hands returned immediately. Even after

breaking and entering and chasing criminals, I did not have the constitution to sneak into a Broadway play. I followed Teeny's lead and seconds later I found myself inside the Neil Simon theater with a smile on my face.

"This lobby is beautiful," I said. "Look at this Oriental rug. And the crown molding. And —"

"Yeah, yeah. We get it. Interior designer. Come on. Let's get our seats." Teeny hurried over toward a staircase and climbed the stairs, her short legs taking the steps two at a time.

Miss May glanced over at me with a smile. "Have you ever seen *CATS*?"

I shook my head. "No. I think I'm excited."

The three of us settled into some empty seats in the back row of the theater. Even all the way up there, I could feel the energy in the room. A little girl in the row in front of us meowed like a little cat at her brother. He meowed back. Beside them, an older woman read her playbill. And I could see ushers escorting ticket holders down at the orchestra level.

I applauded as hard as I could when the curtains opened. Then the play began.

What can I say about *CATS*? What a strange production.

I wasn't sure what to expect from the second half of the show, nor did I have any clue what had transpired in Act I. But as far as I could tell, Act II of *CATS* involved a bunch of people crawling around on stage, singing and acting like cats. There was a magical pile of garbage and some of the cats had magical powers. It was bizarre and wonderful, as all theater should be.

I glanced over at Teeny and Miss May occasionally, and I was delighted to see big smiles on their faces. In my mind, I made a note to take them both to Broadway plays more often. Miss May often talked about how she loved the theater — back when she was an attorney in NYC, she'd gone to Broadway shows at least once a month. We still lived so close to world-class theater, it seemed a shame that we didn't attended a show more often.

Nights out in the big city are always fun with people you love.

At the end of the musical, the actors came out on stage to take a bow. The crowd stood to give the actors a standing ovation and I leaned over to Miss May. "Which one do you think is our guy?"

Miss May squinted to get a better look. "Big, bald dude. Third from the right."

I stood on my toes to get a better look. *Yep.* There was a man standing on stage that exactly fit Edward's description.

"Should we head out and stay near the actors door so we can try to meet him?" I asked.

Miss May shook her head. "Change of plans. If we do that, he'll look at us like annoying fans. He won't give us the time of day. You need to find a way backstage."

I hung my head. "Why me?"

"Because you're young and hot. And you need to convince him that you're a successful theater agent. And you want to represent him."

Teeny leaned forward with a smile. "That's a great idea. Actors love agents. Tell him you'll make him rich. Promise them that you'll break them out of this cat carrier and get him on the big screen."

I groaned. "Do I have to do this?"

Miss May made her eyes wide and sincere. "You don't have to. But if you don't, someone else might get killed real soon."

Teeny grabbed her purse and headed toward the aisle.

"Come on. I'll create a distraction so you can sneak backstage."

I sighed. *Here we go.*

A minute later, we were tiptoeing down to the orchestra level. Teeny took confident strides toward the edge of the stage. I spotted a small staircase off to the side and assumed it led to the backstage area. But two guards stood at the foot of the staircase and I had no idea how Teeny was going to create a distraction big enough to help me get past them unnoticed.

Then Teeny reached the edge of the stage and my question was answered...

Without hesitation, Teeny climbed up on the stage with her elbows then rolled over onto her tummy and slowly climbed to her feet. Once she was standing, she started loudly meowing and running around the stage... Honestly, it was a pretty convincing performance.

The security guards immediately left their post and crossed over toward Teeny. Miss May shoved me over toward the steps. "Now's your chance. Go."

I hurried over toward the staircase. I slipped up the stairs and seconds later, I was backstage at the Neil Simon theater. I threw one last look back at Teeny and the security guards before I went further backstage.

Miss May had joined them and she was speaking in a loud, apologetic tone. "I'm so sorry. My sister is losing her marbles. She thinks she's an actor in this play."

Teeny crossed her arms. "I don't think I'm an actor. I think I'm a cat."

I shook my head and slipped backstage as Miss May and Teeny argued with the security guards. I needed to find that big, bald actor. And I needed to find him fast.

I spotted a sign for the dressing rooms, down the long

hall behind the stage. I walked briskly toward it and stopped at a door labeled "male cats." Seconds later, I was inside a long, narrow space I can only assume was a dressing room for the male cats. One of the walls was lined with mirrors and lithe men prowled everywhere, in various states of feline undress. I shielded my eyes to avoid seeing anything private and took a few steps into the room.

"Ace? Is Ace in here? Hello? I'm looking for Ace?" I tried to project my voice but the men were so loud I knew they couldn't hear me. Then I spotted the big, bald guy in the far corner of the room. I took a deep breath and approached.

I remembered Miss May and Teeny's advice as I approached the actor. "Pretend you're an agent. Say you'll take him to the big screen."

I summoned my most agent-esque personality, which was somewhere between Lucille Ball and Erin Brockovich. I smiled big and approached with my hand outstretched for a handshake. "Hey. How are you? Fantastic performance out there. You are incredible."

The man shook my hand and narrowed his weirdly cat-like eyes. "I'm sorry. Who are you?"

"Who am I? I'm Ashley. Elizabeth. Ashley Elizabeth Morrison. Top agent at the best agency. We need to talk."

The bald man sat a little taller and smiled. "Cool. You're an agent. Awesome. I've been thinking about changing representation."

"Good. Because I've got a big vision for you. I can make you so much money. I'm talking movies. Commercials. Advertisements for cat food."

The man grunted. "You want me to be in cat food commercials?"

"Not if that's not what you want, man. My vision for your future is your vision for your future. Dream your wildest dream, multiply it by fifteen, that's where I'm standing. Waiting for you. With a pile of money. Standing on top of the mountain of success."

The man turned down the sides of his mouth in approval. "I like the way that sounds."

"I'm sure you do." Suddenly, I remembered my mission. I had fallen too deep into character, like Master Skinner. I needed to snap out of it and find out some useful information about Adam. *How can you possibly transition from super-agent to super-sleuth without raising suspicions?* "By the way, so sorry to hear about your former costar Adam Smith. Couldn't believe he was shot during that community theater production of *Phantom of the Opera.*"

"Wasn't that insane?"

"I know you and Adam didn't like each other but still... I wanted to offer my condolences before we talk more business."

The man shook his head. "What are you talking about? I loved Adam."

"Oh," I said. "I must be confused. Are you not Ace?"

The man shook his head and pointed across the room. "That's Ace. He and Adam were mortal enemies."

I spun around to look at where the man had pointed. There, across the room, stood another incredibly tall, incredibly muscly actor with a bald head, wearing a catsuit. He was huge and intimidating. And it was my job to find out if he had killed Adam Smith.

Even worse? I'd used all my agent mojo on the wrong guy.

Ace saw me staring and took a few steps toward me. "What are you looking at?"

"This lady says she's an agent," said the first man. "I

think she thought I was you. Watch out though. I think she might work for a cat food company."

I shook my head. "No. I'm not here about cat food. I'm just... Um... I'm actually not an agent either. I'm just a friend of Adam Smith's. I want to ask you a few questions about him."

Ace narrowed his eyes and looked from me, to the other actor, then back to me. After fifteen seconds of silence, he finally spoke.

"I need to eat. You're buying."

## 27

## ACTING FAST

*A*ce barely took the time to greet Teeny and Miss May before he charged down the block toward what he called "his favorite spot."

"Walk fast. Don't walk like tourists. Stay close or get lost. And I won't come back for you. I need to eat. Every time after I perform I go to this restaurant. The three of you won't compromise my routine."

Miss May took enormous steps to keep up with Ace. Teeny and I both had to break into a light jog to maintain the pace. Short legs don't make big strides.

"You city people love to get places fast," said Teeny.

Ace looked back at her. "You've got that right. And once we get there, we can't wait to leave. It's a beautiful thing. Life operating at maximum efficiency."

"So you said you knew Adam Smith?" asked Miss May.

"Can't walk and talk at the same time. Need to stay focused and determined. I'll tell you everything you want to know once we get there."

Miss May looked over at me. Neither of us had much practice dealing with difficult actors. I tried to look at it like a fun new challenge. But I could tell Miss May and Teeny were running out of patience for Ace's real-life theatrics.

"Is it a far walk?" Teeny asked. "Because if we're going to keep moving at this pace I'm going to need you to pick me up and carry me. Which, by the looks of your tree-trunk arms, you could easily do."

Ace pointed up ahead. "See that hotel? *The New Yorker*?"

"It's fifty stories tall and has a sign on top that says *The New Yorker* in giant letters," I said. "Hard to miss."

"Good. You see it." Ace turned to me. "The restaurant we're going to is on the ground floor of that building. On the corner. It's called the *Tick-Tock Diner* and it's been there since the 1950's."

Miss May nodded. "Sounds charming."

"It's incredibly charming," said Ace. "Us New Yorkers walk fast but we don't accept anything less than the best. And if you know the right places to go, the big city can be just as cozy as any small-town in America."

Ace crossed to the door of the *Tick-Tock Diner* and held it open for us. "Please. After you."

Ace was right. The inside of the diner had incredible charm. There was a classic black and white checkered diner floor. A row of chrome booths lined the far wall. And waiters and waitresses were dressed in all white, just like from a movie about the 50's.

An elderly Greek man sat on a stool behind the counter. He climbed to his feet when he spotted us, came out from behind the counter and gave Ace a hug.

"Ace. So good to see you. How was the show tonight? You were incredible, I'm sure."

Ace laughed. "It went well. Great audience. But I'm hungry."

The Greek man smiled. "You always are."

Moments after we got settled in our booth, before we'd even thought about ordering, the old man brought over a dozen plates of hot, fresh food. Ace laughed when he saw the spread. "Nicholas. This is too much."

The man waved him away. "You bring friends to my restaurant, I want them to see how much we love you here. I bring you all my specialties. Disco fries, Western omelette, big plate of pancakes, onion rings, three milkshakes, everything."

Teeny smiled. "I was hoping those giant cups contained milkshakes. Any chance you can bring some sprinkles on the side?"

Nicholas smiled wide. "For a friend of Ace, you have all the sprinkles in my restaurant."

The man hurried away. Teeny smiled and rubbed her hands together. "This is my kind of restaurant." She grabbed a fry and added, "Mmm. These fries are amazing."

Ace squirted a big pile of ketchup onto the plate. "I told you, us New Yorkers don't accept anything less than the best."

Miss May rolled her eyes. "You know, we're New Yorkers too. We've all lived in the city at one point or another, and you can be in our little town in less than two hours on the train."

"Those two hours make a world of difference," said Ace.

Miss May chuckled. "OK. Good point. It's a little different pace of life. But I still only accept the best."

Ace turned to me. "I don't know anything about you, other than that you knew Adam Smith. And you pretended to be an agent for some reason."

I stammered. "Yes. I did pretend to be an agent. Because... The truth is..."

Teeny leaned forward. "Chelsea is a reporter. She runs

our town newspaper. She's writing a story about Adam Smith. Of course she wanted to get some quotes from his friends on Broadway."

"Adam and I had a...complicated relationship," said Ace.

I pulled a small notebook and pen out of my purse, a gesture I'd picked up from Pine Grove's actual reporter, Liz. "That's interesting. Do you mind if I write some of this down for my story?"

"That's fine." Ace ate a fry. "But don't ask me to repeat anything. I don't repeat myself for journalists. Get it right the first time or don't run the quote."

I gulped. "Got it." *I could never be a real reporter*, I thought. Too much stress. And the stakes were too high. "Go on."

Ace sat back and looked up and to the left a little as he remembered. "Adam and I first met during an acting class, years ago. I don't know if any of you are familiar with the entertainment industry but here's the truth... Most actors are terrible. I don't say that to be mean. It's a sad fact, but 99% of actors in New York or Los Angeles or London... They're just after the fame. The spotlight. The money. They don't have talent."

"Is that what you thought about Adam?" Teeny asked, getting into the gossip.

Ace shook his head. "Quite the opposite. I first took notice of Adam Smith because he was the only other talented actor in that class. We always tried to team up together to be scene partners so we wouldn't have to read with one of the wet fish who called themselves our class-mates. Our scenes were incredible. It was beginner stuff but I remember two or three times we moved the teacher to tears."

"Impressive." Miss May sipped one of the milkshakes. "Tell us more."

"Yeah," said Teeny. "I thought you hated Adam Smith. Mortal enemies. Let's get to that."

"The hatred didn't come for years. For the first decade I knew Adam, neither of us found any work. We went out to the same auditions and neither of us ever got the part. After every rejection, we would meet up and drink wine and complain about how talentless everyone else was. That was fun. Then we both found a little success. At first, that was nice. Until we were competing for the exact same roles. If Adam got a role I wanted, it was painful. And if I got a role Adam wanted, he would yell and scream and cry and treat me like one of those talentless other losers on Broadway."

My eyes bulged. "That's harsh."

"I thought journalists were supposed to be non-biased and nonjudgmental," said Ace.

"The story I write will present the facts in a clear and concise manner. As a person I still have opinions. And that sounded a little harsh."

"Fine. You're right. It was harsh. But it was the truth."

"So the two of you became competitors and that ruined your friendship?" Miss May asked.

"More or less," said Ace.

Teeny leaned forward. "Was a tiny part of you happy when you found out what happened to Adam?"

Ace gasped. "Of course not. That's disgusting. When I learned Adam had been shot on stage... The news devastated me. Adam was a great friend to me for years. After that, yes, he was my competitor. But his greatness drove me to try harder and compelled me to always improve myself as an actor. When he gave up and moved to that little town upstate... It didn't make me feel good. You never want to see someone you came up with retreat like that."

"Pine Grove is wonderful," said Teeny. "Maybe he was just ready to get out of the rat race."

Ace let out a small laugh. "No one thinks of this business as a rat race if you experience real success. When Adam left New York, it was a sign he had given up. Like I said, that made me sad. When I heard he had been murdered..."

Ace looked down. He brought a hand to his forehead and rubbed his temples. He let out a stifled sob.

Miss May looked over at me. I could tell she was wondering... Was Ace really crying? Or was this a performance?

Miss May reached out and took Ace's hand in hers. "I'm so sorry for your loss."

Teeny nodded. "We all are."

"Yep," I added.

I was sorry for Ace's loss, yes, but I was also keenly aware that Miss May, Teeny, and I were there on a mission. Ace had not provided an alibi. He remained a suspect in the murder of Adam Smith. And we needed to gather more information before he left that diner.

I took a deep breath and continued the conversation. "Did you mention how you found out Adam had been killed?"

Ace looked up at me. His eyes hardened. "Why are you asking me that?"

I held up my notebook. "The more details I gather the better story I can write."

"I heard from a friend."

I nodded. "I see. And where were you exactly when Adam was killed?"

Ace narrowed his eyes. "That's not relevant." He sat back.

"Why do you need to know where I was when Adam was shot?"

"It's for the story."

"Let me see your press credentials. You said you write for a small-town paper? What was the name of the paper? What's your email address?"

"Um... the paper is the *Pine Grove Gazette,* and my name is uh, Liz—"

Ace stood. "You think I killed Adam Smith? You think I shot him because he stole my roles?"

I tried to remain impartial and poised, like a real reporter would. "No. Of course not."

Miss May stood. "Everybody calm down. Ace: no one thinks you're a killer."

The owner of the restaurant, Nicholas, approached holding a cup full of sprinkles. "Ace. Everything OK here? These ladies giving you a problem?"

"Yes. They're giving me a big problem, Nicholas. I think it's time for them to leave."

Nicholas sat down the bowl sprinkles and turned to us. "I'm so sorry, nice ladies. Ace is my most loyal customer. If he is unhappy with you, I am unhappy with you."

Miss May held up her hands. "I understand."

"You three have ruined my post-show meal." Ace trained his angry glare on me. "And you're far too stupid to be a reporter."

"Why do you say that?" I asked.

"Because I was on stage Friday night for three straight hours. I couldn't have possibly killed Adam Smith."

I nodded. "That's a good point." I turned to Miss May. "We should've thought of that."

Ace pounded his fist on the table. "Get. Out."

I nodded and hurried to the exit. Miss May and Teeny

followed. We reached the door. Then Teeny darted back toward our table and took one last sip of milkshake.

Ace's voice boomed. "Leave."

"Sorry. I love milkshakes."

Seconds later, Teeny, Miss May and I were back on the streets of New York City. But we were not walking fast and determined like locals. Instead, we stood perfectly still, shocked, dumbfounded, and at a total dead-end.

## 28

## LIFE IN THE FAST LANE

*T*he traffic getting out of the city that night was horrendous. We sat in bumper-to-bumper traffic on the Westside Drive for nearly two hours. But the gridlock give us time to process what had happened with Ace and it helped us decide what we should do next in our investigation.

At first, Miss May was hung up on all the time we'd wasted in the city. "We should have stayed in Pine Grove and looked for the killer there. This was a mistake. It was my fault and I feel bad."

Teeny patted Miss May's shoulder. "Don't worry about it. So the theater critic was a red seagull. That happens in every investigation."

"Red herring," I said.

"Whatever," said Teeny. "This whole trip was a red bird of some sort. But at least we saw a play."

"We saw half a play," said Miss May. "And I don't think I understood any of it any better than I did the first time I saw *CATS*."

Teeny wrinkled her brow. "Really? I thought *CATS* was easy to understand."

I leaned forward to get a better look at Teeny. "Go on."

"There were a bunch of cats in a junkyard. They were fighting over garbage. But at the end of the day they realized they should all be happy and share the garbage. There was also a mystical, magical cat and I think he was supposed to be God or something. And God had a wonderful singing voice, I thought."

I laughed. "Yep. Sounds like you understood it perfectly."

Teeny looked over at me. "Whatever, Chelsea. So I didn't summarize it like your fake newspaper would have. But I'm telling you, I understood every second of that play. I'm a cat inside my heart. That's why."

The traffic ahead of us sped up and Miss May sighed with relief. "Finally. I didn't think these cars were ever going to move."

"Get in the fast lane," said Teeny.

"We're fine where we are." Miss May did not move at all.

Teeny crossed her arms. "Come on. I let you drive my car. The least you could do is take my direction when it comes to what lane to be in."

"You didn't let me drive your car," said Miss May. "You asked if I could drive it because you don't like driving at night."

"That's true," said Teeny. "But it's a lot of fun driving my little pink convertible. It's a privilege and you should respect that."

"I agree with Teeny." I leaned back in my seat. "But I also had a great idea just now..."

"What's your good idea?" Miss May asked.

"Let's talk about the case."

Miss May chuckled. "Oh so your good idea is that we should stop bickering about the traffic and solve the stupid murder?"

I shrugged. "Do you have a better idea?"

"What do you girls think we should do next?" Miss May asked.

"What was the plan we went to the *Brown Cow* this morning?" I asked.

"I was going to get a triple hot chocolate with quadruple sprinkles," said Teeny. "But Brian said he couldn't in good conscience do triple hot chocolate so I got double hot chocolate and it was still good."

"I'm not talking about our plans for hot chocolate," I said. "Before we followed the theater critic to New York City, what were we planning to do to continue our investigation?"

Miss May bit her lip. "Last night Zambia came to the farmhouse and admitted she was having an affair with Adam. She said Adam's wife Dorothy had no idea, remember?"

I nodded. "That's right. But that seems a little far-fetched to me. Everyone in town knew that Adam and Zambia had fallen for each other. And Dorothy was really angry at the play that night."

"So let's find out if Dorothy knew about the affair," said Teeny. "If she knew Adam was canoodling with Zambia, that means Dorothy had a strong motive for murder."

Miss May nodded. "That's correct. And if Dorothy murdered Adam that means Zambia might be next."

I groaned. "I hate when these cases start to feel scary."

"They always feel scary. They're murders." Miss May pulled into the left lane and stepped on the gas.

Teeny threw up her hands. "Now you get into the fast lane?"

Miss May looked over at Teeny. "This is a matter of life and death. I don't have a choice."

## 29

## WE'RE NOT IN KANSAS ANYMORE

*D*orothy and Adam shared a beautiful Victorian home about a one-minute walk outside of town. The home was gray with plum trim. It had gorgeous lattice details and a big turret and a wraparound porch big enough to hold fifty people all sipping mint juleps. As if that weren't enough charm for one house, there was also a white picket fence out front. A tongue-in-cheek "Beware of Actors" sign was hung on the fence.

It was almost midnight when Miss May, Teeny, and I arrived. The night was cold. But the moonlight was sharp and bright, and made the large house seem peaceful and inviting.

I slowed as we approached the white picket fence. I placed my hand on Miss May's arm to stop her from walking any further. "Are we sure we want to bother Dorothy right now?"

"I just sped home all the way from the city in Teeny's pink death-mobile. Dorothy might be a killer. No time like the present."

Teeny stepped between us. "I'm with Chelsea. Not sure

this is the smartest move. Dorothy's gonna know we're here on sleuth business."

Miss May sighed. "So the two of you want to go home and sleep?"

Teeny shrugged. "I'll probably have a snack or a cup of tea first. Then I'll put on one of my late-night shows and fall sleep on the couch. I don't like going straight to bed. You know, it's important to unwind after a big day like this."

Miss May shook her head. "We're already here. One of you should have mentioned these hesitations on the drive."

I winced. "Sorry. I saw the sign on the fence and it spooked me." It also reminded me of my own dog, Steve, who was undoubtedly feeling lonely and annoyed that he hadn't had his puppy supper yet.

A light on the porch turned on. It was yellow and eerie and cast long shadows across our faces. Miss May grumbled. "Great. She's awake."

Teeny's eyes widened. "Should we make a run for it?"

A sultry, deep voice rang out from the porch. "Too late to run, baby. I'm awake and I'm ready to talk."

Teeny perked up. "Dorothy. Hiiiii. Sorry to bother you."

Dorothy stepped into the light. I admired her sharp nose and high cheekbones. She had such distinguished features it made me a little jealous. "Please. You are not bothering me. I've been expecting you."

I sighed and pulled out my phone. I surreptitiously sent a quick text to KP: "Sorry but can check on Steve again before you go to bed?" There was no telling how long we might be out now that Dorothy was awake.

Dorothy opened the door to her home and stepped aside for us to enter. The steps creaked as we ascended to the porch. We had no choice but to enter. We were there to talk to Dorothy and Dorothy wanted to talk.

Moments later, we were sitting in a beautiful Victorian drawing room. There was a large, plush rug on the floor and a few puffy armchairs. The walls were decorated with newspaper clippings detailing Adam's success during his time on Broadway.

Dorothy poured each of us a cup of herbal tea, then settled into one of the armchairs to talk. She had a relaxed and confident demeanor. Almost too relaxed. Almost too confident.

"I suppose you girls are here because you think I'm a suspect."

Miss May gave Dorothy a tight smile. "Suspect is a strong word. But it's our habit to always question the spouse of the deceased."

"No need to mince words, May. You want to know if I was aware of Adam's relationship with his costar Zambia offstage?"

Miss May shrugged. "I suppose that would be helpful information."

Dorothy looked away. The moonlight streamed through the window. Her cheekbones looked pronounced and distinct, like she was in a scene in an old black-and-white movie. "Marriage is a funny thing. Not ha-ha funny. More like... Tragically funny. A man and a woman walk into a church. The priest says some stuff in Latin and you're bound together for life. That's the part where the three of you laugh at my funny joke."

I offered a small laugh. Miss May and Teeny joined in. Teeny scooted forward on her seat. "I get the joke, Dorothy. I've been married so many times I know that Latin stuff by heart."

Dorothy did not look back toward us. She kept her eyes trained on the window, so much like a movie star delivering a monologue. "I loved Adam. I was devoted to him. We lived in the city together and I supported his dreams. Worked three jobs so he could have the freedom to go to auditions. Then I agreed to move up here with him and start anew. It wasn't long after that he met Zambia. And the two of them took up together. I realized then I had a very poor intuition when it came to deciding who I could trust."

Dorothy turned to me. "You understand, Chelsea. I know all about how you almost married the wrong man. And that's because you trusted someone who didn't have your best interests at heart. When you looked into his eyes you saw kindness and warmth and you felt safe there."

My jaw dropped. I did not expect Dorothy to bring up Mike. *Why does everyone have to know everything in a small town?*

Dorothy continued. "Don't you know what I mean, Chelsea?"

I swallowed. It seemed Dorothy would not rest until I engaged in the conversation. "I guess I know what you mean. But I don't know that I ever saw much kindness in Mike's eyes. I was with him because I didn't want to be alone, I think. My parents died when I was young. That's why it was so hard for me to move on after what happened with our wedding. But I'm stronger now and I know it was for the best. I'm lucky I didn't end up with him."

Dorothy pointed at me. "Right. You're lucky. You got away. You never had to experience the feeling of devoting yourself to a man and then learning that he's fallen in love with another woman."

I looked down. "I guess that is lucky. I'm sorry that happened to you."

I looked up. Dorothy's mouth was pressed into a flat line. Her hands were white-knuckling the arms of her chair. She seemed tense. Tense like a guilty person might seem tense. Miss May looked over at me and I could see that she felt that vibe too. Dorothy noticed us noticing and relaxed her grip.

"I'm angry. So what?" Dorothy snapped. "Don't look at each other like you think I'm a killer. I'm a woman scorned. And I have fury. But that doesn't make me a murderer."

Teeny shrugged. "If you're so innocent give us an alibi."

Dorothy chuckled. "I'd be happy to. Remember that night at the play? Adam and Zambia shared that long, disgusting kiss, and everyone saw me storm out of the theater?"

Miss May nodded. "I think I do remember that."

"Of course you remember it," said Dorothy. "Everyone remembers it. I made a fool of myself in front of the whole town. Or Adam made a fool of me. What's the difference?"

"I definitely remember it," said Teeny.

"Great," said Dorothy. "Anyway, I didn't go up to the mezzanine and shoot Adam after that. I went straight to *Peter's Land and Sea* and drowned my sorrows in a monumental ocean of whiskey."

Miss May raised her eyebrows. "And the staff at the restaurant saw you there?"

Dorothy nodded. "I'm sure you'll go there and find out. But yes."

Miss May stood to leave. "Thank you for talking to us."

Dorothy stood too. She took Miss May's hand and her voice cracked. "Wait. Before you go..."

Miss May made eye contact with Dorothy. Dorothy continued. "If you're around town and you hear people gossiping about me or even about Adam... tell them... we were happy once. We were in love. I would have never hurt him."

Miss May nodded. "OK. Thank you for the tea."

## 30

## MAYOR MAYOR, TAKE THE FALL

*T*he next morning, I took Steve out for an extra-long walk around the farm. He was one grumpy puppy, and I couldn't blame him. Miss May and I hadn't been around nearly as much as we should have been. Steve had seen plenty of KP. But he wanted attention from me and Miss May, and he deserved it.

As I meandered through the muddy grounds, between apple trees, fir trees, and all sorts of other trees, I heard another grumpy voice mumbling from nearby.

"KP?" I called out. "Is that you?"

"Yeah," the gruff voice called back. "It's me and this here little-bitty horse."

I passed through a thicket of trees and sure enough, there was KP with See-Saw. I'd known KP forever, but for some reason on that particular day it struck me how sturdy and dependable he was. With his thick dark hair and broad frame, he didn't look a day older than the age he claimed to be — which had been 29 or 39 for the past fifteen years. He liked to change the decade occasionally, depending on his mood. *OK, maybe he looked a few days older than 29.* But in his eyes and his smile, he was still youthful and mischievous, and I couldn't imagine thinking of him as an old man.

"How's it going?" I asked, as Steve playfully rushed up and tried to play with an unreceptive See-Saw.

"Ah," KP grumbled. "The little pony's mad at me. You and May have been out so much, I've been splitting my time between that limpy dog and this ol' girl. She doesn't care for it when I don't pay enough attention to her."

I grinned. "Poor See-Saw. She's not the only cute animal on the farm anymore." As if to prove my point, Steve rolled over, his tongue lolling, and sneezed an adorable, squeaky sneeze.

See-Saw snorted and KP patted her on the head. "She'll be alright," he said. Steve popped up and started to lick See-Saw's short leg. See-Saw looked down at him thoughtfully but didn't move away. I liked to think in her heart of hearts, See-Saw couldn't help but admit Steve was pretty cute.

After a few more minutes of Steve trying to frolic with See-Saw and See-Saw gently rebuffing him, KP and I parted ways and Steve and I went back to the farmhouse.

Miss May was waiting for me by the front door, ready to go over to *Peter's Land and Sea* to verify Dorothy's alibi. I gave Steve his breakfast, which he finished before I'd even left the kitchen. Then I headed out to the VW bus and Miss May chunked the car into gear.

We were both pretty groggy from our late night the previous evening, so we didn't make a lot of small talk on our way into town. But details of the investigation swirled through my mind like cows in a Kansas tornado, and finally I couldn't take it — I had to start speaking my thoughts out loud.

"It would be weird if Dorothy were lying about this alibi."

Miss May turned up the hill that led toward *Peter's Land and Sea.* "I agree. If she wasn't actually there, no one on Petey's staff is going to lie to us about it."

"I suppose it's still good to do our due diligence."

Miss May nodded. "Exactly. Dorothy seemed...off last night. She's seemed a little off the whole time I've known her, in fact. And we should never underestimate any of our suspects."

"I know," I said.

"That's part of what makes us such effective sleuths," Miss May said. "That and the fact that we work in such a slow and methodical manner."

I shrugged. "It's slow and methodical until it's not slow and methodical anymore."

Miss May nodded. "That's true. At a certain point the clues begin to pile up, don't they? And then it's like a snowball rolling down a mountain — out of our control."

I visualized a snowball filled with murder weapons and other clues, growing in size as it sped down a steep slope. Weird mental image, but accurate. Sometimes, our investigations picked up so much momentum that they really were unstoppable.

Miss May pulled into the restaurant parking lot and looked around. "Only a couple cars here this morning."

"Park in front." I pointed to the spot near the entrance. "Might as well take the best spot in the parking lot since there's almost no one else here."

Miss May shook her head. "It's too bad. I bet people are staying away from this place because of our investigation. Everyone knows there was drama here between Adam and Germany. I bet you if Dorothy's alibi is true, word has gotten out that she came here during the play. Locals probably think the place has bad juju right now or something."

"Wow. You say juju now?" I asked. Miss May, ever the pragmatist, was not a woman prone to abstract concepts like "juju," "mojo," or "vibes."

Miss May smirked. "Trying it out. We'll see."

We entered the restaurant and looked around. Sure enough, only three tables were occupied. The place was quiet but the sounds of forks and knives on ceramic plates felt deafening.

Petey's uncle, Jefferson Nebraska, approached with a smile. "Ladies. Welcome back."

"Thanks." Miss May looked around the restaurant. "Have things been slowing down around here since what happened to Adam?"

Jefferson let out a deep breath. His exhale was so forceful, I felt like he'd been holding it in for years. "That's right. I hope it blows over, for Pete's sake. The restaurant can't stay open if business is like this."

I chuckled. "Sorry," I said. "Slow business isn't funny. It's just, you said, 'for Pete's sake.'"

Jefferson stared at me blankly. "That's his name. Pete."

"No, I know," I said. "But for Pete's sake... Oh, nevermind."

"I'm sure it's going to turn around," said Miss May, mercifully bailing me out. "The same thing happened up at the orchard when we found a body there. People in town got spooked. But if the place is good, the customers always return. And after awhile, I think the drama actually boosted sales in a weird way. Mystery brings curious onlookers, you know."

Jefferson nodded. "Can I show you ladies to your table?"

"We're not here to eat." Miss May looked both ways to make sure no one was listening. "We're here to talk. Were you working the night Adam Smith was killed?"

Jefferson bristled. "Why are you asking me that? I didn't even know the guy. Suddenly I'm a suspect?"

Miss May give Jefferson a small smile. "No. You're not a suspect. We're here following up on an alibi."

"Oh," said Jefferson. "I was alone on the floor that night. Business was slow because everyone in town was at the performance. But I'd be happy to tell you everything I know."

Jefferson pulled out a couple seats at a nearby table. "Take a seat. Let's talk."

Miss May held up her hand. "We don't need to sit down. To be frank, I only need the answer to one question."

Jefferson raised his eyebrows, waiting for Miss May to continue.

"Was Dorothy Smith here the night of the performance?"

"Let me think," said Jefferson. "Is that the tall women with the sharp features? Very beautiful? High cheekbones?"

Miss May nodded.

"She's aged well," I said. "I hope I have skin like her when I get old. Not that she's old. I'm sorry. You can answer the question. Go ahead."

Once again, Jefferson stared at me blankly. He and I were not on the same wavelength.

"Was Dorothy here on Friday night?" asked Miss May.

Jefferson nodded. "She was here. She ordered a finger lake filled with whiskey. Seemed like she was drowning her sorrows. But for what's it worth, even if her alibi was false, I would still think Dorothy's innocent."

"Really?" Miss May looked at Jefferson over the top of her glasses. "What's your theory?"

Jefferson leaned in and whispered. "Zambia seems guilty, if you ask me."

"Have you noticed her doing anything suspicious?" Miss May asked.

Jefferson scoffed. "I've always been suspicious of Zambia. May, you've live here forever, right? Don't you remember what a mess this town was when she was mayor?"

Miss May closed her eyes for a few seconds then opened them. "I remember."

Jefferson turned to me. "Zambia was the worst mayor in the history of mayors. She was sketchy and untrustworthy. Living here during her time in office was horrible."

"That's very extreme," snapped Miss May. "No need to dredge up such ancient history, alright?"

"Wow. Sorry." Jefferson took a step back from Miss May. "You don't need to get snippy with me."

Miss May sighed. "No. I'm sorry. I've got a lot on my mind. And I just... I know Zambia wasn't perfect as mayor... but I don't want to talk about it."

A party of five entered the restaurant and waited by the host stand. Jefferson noticed them and acknowledged them with a small nod. "Got any more questions? If not, I should seat these people."

"No more questions. Thank you for your help."

Miss May looked after Jefferson as he limped over to help the party of five. My aunt was distracted and lost in thought. I put my hand on her shoulder.

"Are you OK? Why'd you get so upset about Zambia?"

"Nothing. It's fine." Miss May brushed off her coat and exited the restaurant in a hurry. I looked after her. Something was wrong and I needed to figure out what.

## 31

## OLD NEWS

*A*s we exited *Peter's Land and Sea,* I could practically see a dark cloud hanging over Miss May's head. Her mouth was in a deep frown, her hands were clenched, and her stride was brisk and stiff.

I wanted to know why my aunt had gotten so upset in the restaurant when Jefferson brought up Zambia's term as mayor. But Miss May wasn't in the mood to talk. She dismissed my concern and insisted that nothing was wrong. When I pressed her, she awkwardly changed the topic.

She told me she had forgotten to take care of some important business at the orchard. I protested, but Miss May insisted that we had to get back to the farm pronto so that she could have an emergency meeting with KP.

When we got home, Miss May disappeared into her office and buried her head in the computer. But I couldn't stop thinking about what had happened back at *Peter's Land and Sea.* There was more to the story of Zambia's time as mayor of Pine Grove. And I wanted to find out what it was. If I was a cat, my curiosity would definitely be killing me.

I poked my head into Miss May's office with a small

smile. "I'm going to head to town for a cup of coffee. Do you want anything?"

Miss May barely looked up from her computer. "I'm fine. Just made a mistake with the crop rotation this year. Need to figure out which apples we're harvesting and when. I'm sure it's going to work out. Sorry I'm cranky."

"OK. And we'll talk about the investigation later?"

Miss May nodded. "Have fun in town."

I headed out to the driveway, where I hoisted myself up into my light blue pickup truck. I hadn't done a ton of driving before moving back to Pine Grove, so this truck almost felt like my first car, and I had a deep affection for it.

As I drove to the *Brown Cow*, I thought about Miss May's demeanor. I'd only seen her get secretive like this a handful of times, and usually it was about her status with the New York State Bar Association, or...about my parents. I knew from Detective Wayne Hudson that my aunt had long suspected my parents' death was not purely accidental. She'd done some digging back around the time that they died, but she never spoke to me about that. I wondered what was going on with her now...

I parked absentmindedly on the street and ambled into the *Brown Cow*. I ordered my cup of coffee but didn't make much small talk with Brian while I waited. I was too caught up in my own thoughts. Across the street I noticed Liz, the editor of the *Pine Grove Gazette*, entering her office.

I approached Liz's office quietly and announced my presence with a small knock. She was sitting behind her sturdy, oak desk, as I expected she would be.

"Chelsea. Where is Miss May?"

"Orchard business."

Liz slowly closed her laptop. "Are you here to talk about

your investigation? I'd rather not consult with you unless Miss May is here."

"I'm not here to talk about the case. At least... I don't think so."

Liz raised her eyebrows. "Is this a social call? I never thought you liked me. Most people don't like me until they get to know me. Then they love me forever. Especially men. Sometimes it can be a burden."

I shifted my weight. The truth was, I did like Liz, but she was kind of intimidating. "This isn't quite a social call, either. I do like you, though. You're weird in a good way."

Liz nodded. "Thank you. So are you. What can I help you with?"

"I'm wondering if you have any information about Pine Grove back in the 90's... When Zambia was mayor."

"Zambia. So this <u>is</u> about your investigation."

I shrugged. "I really don't know. Trust me. This is extracurricular, as far as I'm concerned. I never even knew she was mayor until this investigation. But people keep being weird about it."

"As you know, Chelsea, you and I are the same age. I wasn't around when Zambia was mayor, either. I mean, I was around. But I wasn't paying attention. I've tried to learn about those years in our town but the bookkeeping was horrendous. Most of the newspapers from then were never digitized and I can't find the files."

I hung my head. "So there's no official record of Zambia's term as mayor?"

"Unfortunately, no. But I think I can connect you with the next best thing..."

Liz smirked, stood and pulled on her jacket. "Follow me."

Ten minutes later we were standing in the vestibule of

*Grandma's,* Teeny's restaurant. Teeny smiled and rushed over to give me a hug. "Chelsea. Long time, no see. Where is Miss May?"

I shook my head. "Nobody wants to hang out with me if I'm by myself."

"That's not true," said Teeny. "It's just... I'm not sure I've ever seen you by yourself before. You two are like peas in a bod."

*Peas in a pod,* I thought, but I kept it to myself.

"We're here conducting research," said Liz. "Research about the history of Pine Grove." Liz stood on her tippy-toes and scanned the seating area of the restaurant. "Is Humphrey at his table?"

Teeny smiled. "Yup. And he's not going to leave for another four hours, at least. Got Semolina the hound dog hiding under there, too. He thinks I don't know he brings his dog. I know. Come on. Follow me."

Humphrey, a grouchy old man with a droopy old hound dog named Semolina, was one of Teeny's regulars. Humphrey had been a suspect in our last investigation, mostly because of his strong desire to hold the position as the town's Santa Claus. *But that's a whole other story.*

As we crossed the restaurant, Liz explained that Humphrey had worked as the editor of the *Gazette* in the 90's. She assured me that Humphrey would know more about Zambia's time as mayor than anyone else.

Teeny led us over to Humphrey's table in the back corner of the restaurant. He was asleep, with his head down on a newspaper. A puddle of drool leaked out the corner of his mouth and he snored loudly.

"He's been asleep for about an hour," said Teeny. "Good luck waking him up."

Teeny hurried back into the kitchen. Liz gestured at

Humphrey like he was a five-star meal. "OK. That man right there knows everything that happened in Pine Grove in the 90's."

Humphrey sat straight up and wiped the drool from his mouth. I yelped, startled by the suddenness of his awakening. Liz pressed her hand to her chest and laughed.

"I don't know everything," Humphrey said, as alert as if he'd been mid-conversation with us. "What's the big idea? Why are you interrupting my nap?"

Liz kept laughing. "Humphrey! You scared us."

"You scared me, right out of a deep sleep!" Humphrey glared at me. "Where's Miss May?"

"She's back at the farm," said Liz. "And Chelsea doesn't appreciate that no one wants to hang out or talk to her unless Miss May is around."

"I didn't say that," I said. I took a step toward Humphrey. "Is it OK if we sit for a second?"

"Sure. Sit."

Liz and I slid into the booth across from Humphrey. I heard Semolina grunting and licking her lips beneath the table. I assumed we'd probably interrupted her nap too.

"So you're here to pick my brilliant brain about ye old Pine Grove? What do you want to know?"

"I was hoping you could tell me something about Zambia's term as mayor," I said. "It came up earlier and Miss May acted a little odd. Did something happen when Zambia was mayor? Was there a scandal? Something like that?"

Humphrey wrinkled his face even more than its natural state, which was pretty wrinkled. "Did you just find out Zambia was mayor of Pine Grove?"

I nodded. "Yeah."

"That's weird."

I looked over at Liz. She shrugged. "Weird? Why is that weird?"

Humphrey took a big bite of bacon. "Because Zambia was your parents' best friend. They were basically the reason she got elected."

The blood drained from my face. I felt dizzy. I put my palms face down on the table to steady myself. I wasn't sure why, but for some reason, learning such a significant detail about my parents stunned me. "Was Zambia mayor when..."

Humphrey nodded. "That's right. Zambia was mayor of Pine Grove when your parents died."

## 32

## HORSING AROUND

*I* attempted to squeeze Humphrey for more information but he had a "bathroom emergency" and had to leave the table. Then I headed back to the kitchen to talk things over with Teeny but she was too busy putting out a literal fire to chat.

Teeny's cooking was consistently delicious, but her kitchen was on fire more than one might expect. When I went back to my booth, Liz was on the phone with a source for another story. She held up her finger like, "We'll talk in one minute," but I could tell her call was going to take a while.

I looked around the restaurant. A young couple played with their baby. Teenage boys threw French fries at one another. Everyone was having a good time but I felt all alone.

Alone without Teeny. Alone without Miss May. Alone without my parents. I needed a friend, and there was only one place left to turn. Only one unconditional, loyal, steadfast listener, and I knew she would be there for me in my time of need.

I was talking, of course, about See-Saw.

I entered the barn about twenty minutes later with a small smile on my face. Steve padded behind me, contentedly sniffing around the bundles of hay.

See-Saw was busy devouring a big bucket of food, her tail wagging. I laughed when I saw her. She had such a peaceful energy, even when she was annoyed or jealous or eating. Her big horse eyes spotted me and she whinnied.

I pulled up a stool and sat beside See-Saw as she ate. "Hey girl. Do you remember my parents? I don't know if you came to the farm before or after they... Well, anyway..."

See-Saw kept eating.

"My dad was big and tall. I remember walking through the apple trees on this orchard, sitting on his shoulders. He had salt-and-pepper hair that always smelled like baby powder. And his jean jacket was the softest thing I've ever touched."

See-Saw looked up at me, then turned back to her food. I appreciated her patience and gave her a nice pat on the back. Steve wandered over, licked my leg in a comforting gesture, then continued exploring the many smells in the barn.

"My mom was the most beautiful woman I've ever seen. A lot of people think their mothers are beautiful. I guess that's kind of narcissistic. But I don't just think that because my mom had pretty hair or pretty eyes or a pretty smile. We spent so much time together when I was a kid... I'm talking about her spirit, her energy. Those were the things that made her beautiful. She was curious and smart and hardworking. And she was so funny. She would chase me around the house, pretending to be a monster, for hours. When there was a thunderstorm, we'd build a tent in the living room and we would hide inside, shrieking whenever the thunder clapped."

See-Saw stomped her foot.

"Don't get me wrong, Miss May is incredible. She's a second mother to me and always has been. But she hasn't talked to me much about my parents, so all I have are my memories. Like... Why didn't Miss May tell me Zambia was so close with my parents when they were alive? Zambia is such a big part of this investigation. She might have memories of my parents that would help me understand them even more. I want to know those things. I'm hurt that I had to find that stuff out from grumpy Humphrey."

"Hey, Chelsea." Miss May entered the barn with her hands buried in the pocket of a sweat shirt. "Are you OK?"

I nodded. Miss May pulled up a second stool and took the spot beside me, near See-Saw.

"I'm sorry I didn't tell you how close Zambia was with your parents."

"So you heard that."

Miss May nodded. "I suppose I avoid talking about your parents because I avoid thinking about them. Your mother was my sister. My best friend. Me and her and your dad, we were an inseparable trio. But our family has always been private, for better or worse. Growing up, we didn't talk about our feelings. We didn't discuss our family history. We kept our emotions buried and preferred to have fun when we were with one another. I see now... That might be a bad habit. You and I need to have hard conversations, especially about your parents. So I want you to know... After this investigation I'm going to tell you everything I remember about both of them. You can talk to Zambia and everyone else who knew them. Write it all down. Make a journal of memories, if you want. I think it's only right to honor their lives in some way."

Tears flooded my eyes without warning. "That sounds nice," I choked out, struggling to keep the lump in my throat under control. I looked up at Miss May. "Thank you."

Miss May nodded. "Honestly, we could start that conversation now."

I held up my hand. "No. There's a killer in Pine Grove. That has to be our priority. Once the case is solved we can talk about my parents in detail. But I think we have an obligation to catch the killer first."

Miss May rubbed See-Saw's back. "Alright. Let's catch this killer."

Steve ran toward us, barking enthusiastically. I wondered if he was as eager to find the perpetrator as we were.

Either that, or he was just hungry. Hard to tell with dogs.

## 33

# SPRING IS SPRUNG

*E*ven though I had just suggested to Miss May that we wait to find out more information about my parents until our investigation had concluded, I found myself obsessing over them all night. I don't think I got five consecutive seconds of sleep. I tossed and turned in my bed, mind racing, as I imagined all the new facts I might soon learn about my parents.

Miss May had already told me that my mom and dad spent almost every weekend helping out at the orchard. They were definitely a part of the fabric of life in Pine Grove. And I knew there had to be dozens of people in town who'd had interactions with my parents. I didn't care how big or how small those interactions were. I just wanted to find out more. The people of Pine Grove were an untapped resource for me and the thought of discussing my parents openly in town delighted me.

Zambia was chief among those untapped resources. And I was dying to talk to her again. Even though she had a volatile temper and a confrontational vibe, I wanted nothing more than to talk to Zambia. Immediately.

So I snuck out of the farmhouse at around 7 AM and made my way over to Zambia's place.

Steve almost gave me away. He woofed softly as I padded toward the front door. But I put my finger to my lips to shush him and gave him about a dozen treats to buy his silence. It worked.

When I stepped out on the front porch, spring was in the air. A low fog hung over the orchard. Birds chirped. And it had to be almost 60°. This was a wonderful, misty spring morning, one of the warmest days we'd had in months.

I decided to walk over to Zambia's. In part, because I wanted to enjoy the incredible morning. I also wanted to exit quietly and I knew if I drove off in the pickup, Miss May would wake up and wonder where I was going.

As I walked down the steep curves of Whitehill Road toward town, I planned out my conversation with Zambia. Everyone knew Zambia was an early riser, so I was sure she would be up and ready to talk. I figured I would start the conversation by pretending I had run into her by accident.

After a bit of small talk, probably about the beautiful morning, I planned to casually mention my parents. I'd say something like, "My parents loved March mornings." Then I would hang back and see if Zambia volunteered any information about them.

If Zambia did not chime in with a story or anecdote about my parents, I figured I would get more direct. I'd say something like, "You knew my parents, didn't you? I heard the three of you were inseparable for awhile there."

Then Zambia would launch into a story about how wonderful my mom and dad were. Maybe she'd sprinkle in some details about how cute I had been when I was a little girl. She'd invite me inside for a cup of coffee and we'd talk for hours and hours. Probably Zambia would show me pictures of my parents looking radiant and glamorous in Pine Grove. Perhaps she'd even pop in an old video of the three of them talking about life and joking around and drinking red wine until five in the morning.

*OK. All that might have been a bit far-fetched but a girl can dream, right?*

I slowed as I approach Zambia's cute little house.

The place had a spooky appearance that morning. The thick layer of fog surrounded the home like a moat. Sporadic birdsong sounded panicked rather than melodious. And the front door to the house was propped open a few inches.

I walked up the front path one careful step at a time. My eyes were trained on the open door. I felt my chest tighten and wiped my sweaty palms on my pants. When I got to the door, I nudged it open with my foot. "Hello? Zambia?"

I poked my head inside. Particles of dust were suspended in sunlight. A winter coat was draped on the banister. A black and white cat skittered from the foyer up a steep staircase. The cat stopped halfway up the staircase, turned and looked at me.

"Hey there, cutie. What're you looking at?"

The cat meowed. Her big eyes looked scared. She gestured back up the steps with her adorable little head.

"You want me to come upstairs?"

The cat blinked.

"Zambia?" I called out. "This is Chelsea Thomas. Are you home?"

The cat meowed and once again gestured up the stairs. Then the cat turned and pranced up a few steps. I entered and followed.

Each step groaned as I ascended the staircase. I grabbed the banister and it wobbled. *This place is falling apart*, I thought. The banister was loose like it had been leaned on, heavily and repeatedly.

The cat waited for me at the top of the steps. I knelt down and extended my pointer finger. The little cutie rubbed her face against my finger, then turned and headed toward the room at the end of the hall.

"Where you taking me, kitty?"

The cat kept right on walking. I followed. "You taking me to see Zambia?"

The cat meowed again.

"Zambia," I called out. "I'm upstairs. Just playing with your cat. Is everything OK?"

The cat reached the door at the end of the hall and waited for me. I made eye contact with her and nodded. "OK. I'll go in first." *Obviously, since I had opposable thumbs and could open doors.*

I took a deep breath. Then I pushed open the door to Zambia's bedroom... And screamed.

## 34

## SHOCK AND PAWS

Zambia was prone in her bed. She had a pillow over her face. Her body was stiff, twisted into an unnatural position. The bedroom window, which led to a trellis, had been left open. The nightstand had been knocked over. The sheets had been kicked to the floor.

The kitty jumped to the bed. I scooped her up and held her close to my chest. "Oh my goodness. Zambia is... She's been murdered."

The cat meowed.

"You're sticking with me, OK?" I backed toward the bedroom door. "And we're both getting out of this room."

Moments later, I sat at Zambia's kitchen table and called Miss May.

"Hello?" She was groggy. It was barely 8 AM.

"Miss May."

"Chelsea. Where are you?" I could hear Miss May opening her blinds. "Your car is still here."

I absently stroked the cat, who was purring in my lap. "I left. Walked to town. Wanted to talk to Zambia about my parents."

Five seconds of silence.

"What happened, Chelsea?"

"I got to Zambia's. It's so foggy out today. The door was open. It was open...so I went inside."

"OK, Chelsea. You're speaking very slowly. I can tell you're in shock. Everything's OK. Whatever happened. Take a deep breath, OK?"

The cat meowed.

"Did you get a cat?"

I looked down. Kitty's little tail swished on the table. I rubbed her scruff and sighed. "That's Kitty. Or at least, Kitty is what I'm calling her. She must have been Zambia's cat."

"Why are you speaking in the past tense?"

I swallowed. "You know why."

Ten seconds of silence.

"Was it murder?"

I nodded. I knew Miss May couldn't hear my nod, but she'd know by my silence.

"How?"

"She was... She was suffocated. Signs of a struggle. The killer escaped out the window. They may have still been here when I arrived. No way to know for sure. Kitty knew something was wrong. She led me straight to Zambia. She's such a sweet cat."

I heard clanging and banging on Miss May's end of the line.

"Are you getting dressed?"

"Putting on my shoes now. I'm coming to you. Have you called the police yet?"

I shook my head. "No. I called you first."

"Good," said Miss May. "I'll be there in five."

Miss May got there in ten minutes. I met her at the front door and she gave me a big hug. "You're OK."

"I'm glad you're here," I said.

"Have you looked around?"

I shrugged. "No I didn't even think about it. I just sat at the kitchen table. Didn't move until I heard you pull up." I stuck my head out the door. "Still foggy out there."

"I noticed. Surprised the fog hasn't lifted by now." I took one last look at the fog and closed the door behind Miss May as she entered. We had a job to do, and it was time to get serious.

Over the course of the next hour, Miss May, Kitty and I conducted a thorough search of Zambia's house. We were careful not to tamper with anything that could have been evidence. But to be honest, there wasn't much to tamper with.

The basement had already been cleared by the junk removal guys. And it appeared that all the upstairs bedrooms had also been cleared. Most of the rooms of the house, in fact, did not contain much of anything.

After we had searched every room, we stopped in the upstairs hallway to talk. "Zambia was hiding something," said Miss May. "And it was more than evidence of an affair."

I shrugged. "Maybe she was planning to move."

Miss May tilted her head from side to side. "Possible. I thought that. It's also possible these rooms have always been empty. Zambia lives alone so I doubt she had much use for spare bedrooms."

I looked into the empty bedroom behind Miss May. I peered around my aunt's ample frame to get a better look inside. There wasn't a stick of furniture. The room was spotless, in fact. Totally barren.

"I don't know. Even if Zambia did kill Adam... It's not like every item in every single room could have been a piece of evidence."

"She was a strange lady. Maybe that's all there is to it."

"What do you think of the scene of the crime?" I asked. I winced at the gruesome memory.

"I think you're right. There was a struggle. It's clear."

"You think the killer escaped out that open window?"

Miss May shrugged. "It's possible. But you said the front door was open when you arrived, right?"

I nodded.

"Maybe they just left through that the door. And came in through the window. Either way, this crime was committed in a hurry."

"Most likely scenario... Hurried into the front door, then exited out the window when I arrived. That's a chilling thought." I shuddered. It was never fun to realize you had been in the same home as a murderer.

Miss May rubbed my shoulder with her firm, comforting hand. "That's the most likely scenario. Sorry to say."

"Can we draw any other conclusions from the scene of the crime?" I asked.

Miss May nodded. "Zambia was smothered with that pillow. So whoever did this was strong enough to overpower her. But also nimble enough to slip out the window and climb down the trellis. I think we're looking for a male. Probably someone on the younger side."

I nodded. "Good to know. Although it seems Zambia put up a pretty good fight. Possible the killer was a woman, too. And I mean, just to keep all the avenues open...it's possible the window was already open, and the killer entered and exited through the front door."

Kitty approached and rubbed up against Miss May's shins. Miss May squatted down and smiled. "You know who did this, don't you Kitty? You're cute and smart. I can tell."

The cat placed her paws up on Miss May's knee. Miss

May laughed. "Do you want to be picked up you sweet little thing?"

Kitty looked up at Miss May with her big eyes. Miss May shook her head. "This cat has the personality of a dog."

"You have no idea. I walked around holding her in my arms all morning. She didn't squirm and she didn't try to jump. I think at one point she fell asleep."

Miss May nuzzled against Kitty's face. "What do you think, Kitty? What should we do next?"

I crossed to the hallway window and looked out over the driveway. "Maybe we should slip out and call the police anonymously. We don't need Chief Flanagan hating us more than she already does."

Miss May stooped over and placed Kitty on the floor. Kitty immediately rubbed up against my legs. I squatted down to pet her.

"That's a great idea," said Miss May. "Unfortunately, I'm parked right outside. And we live in a small town. So everyone already knows we're here. Half the town is probably already assuming Zambia has been murdered."

I groaned. "So we need to call the police."

Miss May nodded. "I'm surprised they're not already here."

## 35

## SUNSHINE AND WAYNE-BOWS

hief Sunshine Flanagan emerged from Zambia's bedroom with a hard look in her eyes. "Inconclusive."

Miss May thew her hands up. "Inconclusive? That's absurd. Zambia was murdered. It's clear."

"Unless you think the pillow just, fell on her face and she couldn't manage to lift it off," I said. I wasn't normally inclined toward conflict, but Chief Flanagan pushed my buttons.

"Detective Hudson. Why have these women not been detained?"

Wayne poked his head out from one of the empty bedrooms. "What was that?"

Flanagan crossed her arms. "These women should have been detained. I requested that they be detained and questioned."

Wayne's eyes widened and he looked over at me. "Oh. Right. You want me to do that immediately?"

Flanagan nodded.

"You want them to be detained like... I should put them in handcuffs?"

Flanagan rubbed her temples. "No, Wayne. Just take them to an empty bedroom and get the facts."

Miss May gestured toward Zambia's room. "You have the facts. This place is empty. That's a crime scene. Zambia was murdered. Treat this like a murder. Do your job."

I stepped back. Miss May rarely spoke with that kind of force, especially when she was addressing authority. But injustice had away of angering Miss May. I related. Flanagan rubbed us both the wrong way.

"On second thought, maybe you should use the handcuffs," Flanagan turned to Wayne. "If these women keep resisting do whatever you need to do."

Miss May scoffed. "No one is resisting."

A voice yelled up from outside the house. "Hey. What happened?"

Wayne crossed to the hallway window and parted the curtains. The town lawyer, Tom Gigley, stood on the front lawn. With his distinguished posture and shock of white hair, Gigley was unmistakable even from far away. Also unmistakable? There was a mob in the front yard. Twenty townspeople stood behind Gigley, muttering and speculating.

Wayne turned back to Flanagan. "We got a situation on the lawn, Chief."

Tom cupped his hands around his mouth and yelled once again. "I see you, Hudson. What's going on in there? Are Miss May and Chelsea inside? Is everyone OK?"

Flanagan groaned. "Take the job in a small town, they said. It will be quiet, they said. It's a cushy gig, they said. Nothing ever goes wrong in small towns."

Wayne looked over at Flanagan. "Are you OK, Chief? You're talking to yourself."

"Get out of the way, Detective." Flanagan crossed to the window and opened it. "Attention townspeople. This is your Chief of Police speaking."

"We can see that," said Gigley. "We all know you're the Chief, Chief."

Brian from the *Brown Cow* stepped out of the crowd. "Yeah. Why did you announce that? We all know you."

"OK. Sorry." Flanagan stuck her head out the window. Her luxurious red hair fell around her shoulders like a beautiful ginger waterfall. "This is an official police investigation. Please step off the property."

"We want to know what's going on," said Tom. "Zambia is my neighbor. I have a key to her house. I have a right to be here."

Flanagan grabbed her walkie-talkie. "Can I get back-up to Zambia's house?"

A voice came back over the walkie-talkie. "Sure thing, Chief. And this is Zambia who?"

The chief sighed. "Zambia. The only woman named Zambia in town."

Gigley called back up. "You don't even know her last name? That's a disgrace. Our population is so small. You're supposed to protect us and know all of us by name."

"Of course I know her last name," said the chief. "It's... It's..."

Wayne leaned in and whispered in Flanagan's ear. She nodded. "Baker. Zambia Baker."

"Wayne just told you that," said Tom. Flanagan grumbled under her breath, then forced a smile and a wave. "OK. Thank you all for your help."

Miss May leaned forward. "Chief. If you need a little

help, why don't you send us outside? Chelsea and I can talk to the townspeople. We'll tell whatever story you want us to tell. The crowd will be comforted when they see that we're OK."

Flanagan slammed the window closed and turned to Miss May. "Out of the question. You still have to give an official report."

"We're going to say it was a murder," said Miss May. "And you need to say the same. As a matter of fact, that's what I'm going to tell the townspeople whenever I get out of here. This was a murder and your Chief of Police has no sense of urgency."

Flanagan clenched her teeth. "You two. Always so quick to cry murder. Let me do my job and stop jumping to conclusions."

I scowled. "It doesn't take a detective to reach the conclusion that Zambia was murdered. Anyone with eyes could see that."

The chief grunted. "It seems to me that there are a number of possibilities. Maybe she slept funny. I don't know."

Miss May and I crossed our arms in unison. We glared at Flanagan. The chief slumped over.

"Fine. I'm going to investigate this as a crime. Happy?"

Miss May tapped her foot. "Why would I be happy? I just want justice for a woman I've known my entire life. All you want is to move on from the murder of a woman whose last name you only just learned."

"I knew it was Baker. I'm just stressed. It was on the tip of my tongue."

Miss May shook her head. "Sure."

Flanagan licked her lips. She raised her finger and started to say something, then stopped herself. "No. I'm not

going to engage with you right now. You amateur sleuth."
Flanagan said amateur sleuth like it was a dirty word.
"Wayne. Interview them. Now."

Wayne nodded, then led me and Miss May down the
stairs.

A minute later, I was back at the kitchen table. I held
Kitty on my lap. Miss May sat beside me. Wayne sat across
from us, detective notebook open. He asked the normal
questions. And I told him the truth.

"I found out Zambia had been a good friend of my
parents. So I came here to talk to her. I've been feeling a lot
lately like I want to know more about them."

Wayne accepted my answer. He was patient and calm
throughout the conversation. It might have been the first
time ever that he didn't subtly imply that Miss May and I
somehow did something wrong by discovering the body.

Once Wayne had finished questioning us, Miss May and
I said our good-byes and headed toward the door, then Miss
May turned back. "Wayne. Make sure Flanagan takes this
seriously. The killer is still out there."

Wayne hissed through his teeth. "Let's stay way from
words like killer until the investigation is closed."

Miss May sighed. "Zambia was Adam's costar in the play.
They clearly knew each other very well. Now they're both
dead. Zambia did not die of natural causes."

"However she died, we'll find out," Wayne said, his
patience waning.

I shrugged. "Unless we find out first."

## 36

## TARTING OVER AGAIN

*M*iss May and I went straight to Teeny's restaurant for breakfast. We were hungry, sure. But we also knew that Teeny would be even hungrier for information. She had no doubt heard about the crowd at Zambia's house. And we knew Teeny must have been dying to see us, no pun intended. *I hate that pun.* Hard to avoid when you're constantly investigating murders, though.

Teeny rushed up and hugged us as soon as we entered *Grandma's.* "Can't believe you two found another dead body without me. That is so frustrating. Also, so sorry to hear about Zambia. Should have led with that."

Miss May shook her head. "It was terrible. Chelsea discovered the scene on her own."

Teeny clucked her tongue. "Poor Chelsea. You're always finding dead bodies. That must be hard for you."

I slumped against the wall. "Now that you mention it, yeah. It is hard for me. Stressful. Exhausting."

Teeny leaned in. "I hear the cops are trying to pass this one off as an accident. Come on. And Flanagan didn't even know Zambia's last name?"

Miss May shrugged. "Everyone was shocked by that but it made sense to me. Zambia was like Madonna. She went by one name in this town."

Teeny shook her head. "No. If you're going to be Chief of Police in a town this tiny, you need to know everyone's last name. You need to know everyone's mother. And if you don't know the name of their pets, you should be fired."

Miss May chuckled. "Small town logic at its finest. I like that."

Teeny nodded over toward our usual booth. "Come on. I've got a fresh batch of tarts that need to be eaten."

Sure enough, a plate of tarts was already waiting on our table. Miss May cringed when she saw them. "This is a little depressing, considering how Adam died."

"I still think it's pretty bizarre that he decided on such a tart-based interpretation of *Phantom of the Opera*," I said.

Teeny nodded. "I know. But they're so delicious. I couldn't resist whipping up an extra batch. I felt bad while they were in the oven. Then I ate one and I felt better. Then I felt bad again because I ate seven."

Miss May laughed and bit into a tart. "They are good."

I leaned forward to get a better look. "Strawberry filling this time?"

Teeny pointed at me. "You know it, beautiful. Yum, Yum. But enough about the tarts..." Teeny flattened her palms down on the table. "Let's talk suspects."

Miss May shrugged. "OK."

"You two discussed suspects without me, didn't you?" Teeny said, detecting Miss May's ambivalence. "That is so annoying. I'm part of this team. I'm valuable. Neither of you watch the mystery shows. I watch every mystery show, I know all the classic plots, all the twists and turns, and I know how these people think. That's it. I'm taking the tarts away."

Miss May pulled the plate of tarts close to her torso. "We didn't discuss the suspects without you. Relax. We just talked about the general type that we might be looking for."

Teeny held up her hands. "And? What's the general type?"

"We think the killer escaped out the window," I said. "So it was probably a skinny man or a woman."

"Most likely a man," said Miss May. "Because they also overpowered Zambia with the pillow."

Teeny covered her mouth with her hands. "The poor woman was smothered with a pillow?! Horrific. Were there signs of struggle?"

I nodded. "Great question. There were absolutely signs of a struggle. So I think it could have been a woman too, because it looked like Zambia put up quite a fight."

Teeny nodded. "So it's just someone who could fit through a window, basically. That's who we're looking for."

"Or a door," I said. "The front door was also open."

Teeny rolled her eyes. "Well what other clues do we have? The sign-in book?"

"No, you were right," I said begrudgingly. "That was a dead-end. I don't think anyone has signed into that thing in years."

"What else?" Teeny asked.

I took another bite of tart. The powdered sugar spilled onto my chin and dusted my shirt. That strawberry really was delicious. "I don't know. I think it would be smart for us to circle back to the suspects we'd already discussed, prior to Zambia's death. Seems to me we're probably looking for the same killer. That's usually the case in our cases."

"True. It almost always is," said Teeny.

"Master Skinner is a good suspect," said Miss May. "But we already learned he was being painted by Daisy Johnson at the time of the murder."

"And Dorothy has an alibi too. She was pounding back whiskey at *Peter's Land and Sea* at the time Adam Smith was shot," I said. "Jefferson Nebraska confirmed it."

Teeny licked the strawberry filling off of her tart. "Do you have any other options? What about Petunia? She has an obvious gambling problem. Maybe Zambia owed her money."

"That's a stretch," said Miss May. "We're looking for someone who had motive to kill both Adam and Zambia. You think they might have both owed her so much cash she was willing to kill?"

"Yeah, that seems unlikely," I said. "Also, could Petunia really have climbed out that window with no problem?"

Miss May shrugged. "She could have just used the front door, remember?"

"Ugh," I said. "We're getting nowhere."

Miss May leaned forward. "I keep coming back to Dorothy."

"Jefferson said he saw her at the restaurant," I said. "I don't like the guy, and he clearly doesn't like me, but I don't know why he'd lie to protect Dorothy."

Teeny sat straight up. "I have an idea. What if Zambia was a secret government agent. It sounds crazy, I know. But the government has secret agents, right? We can all agree on that. So why couldn't it have been Zambia?"

Miss May's throat rumbled with skepticism. "Where is this going, Teeny?"

Teeny shrugged. "I don't know. That's all I've got. What if Zambia was a secret government agent? If that's true, we get a whole new pool of suspects. The Russians, for instance.

The Russians love to kill government agents. They do it all the time. It's a Russian pastime."

Miss May laughed. "OK. We'll keep that in mind."

Teeny nodded, pleased with herself. "Very well. Thank you."

I felt my phone buzz in my pocket. I pulled it out to see who was calling me. "It's the police station."

"Answer it," said Miss May.

I nodded and picked up the call. "Hello?"

"This is the Pine Grove Police Department. You have an incoming collect call from Germany Turtle. Do you wish to accept?"

"Yes, I'll accept the call." I made eye contact with Miss May and mouthed, "Germany has been arrested!"

## 37

## TURTLE SOUP

*P*ine Grove, New York has one single jail cell, in the back of the modest police department. Over the course of our previous investigations, we'd ended up visiting a lot of our friends and family in that single cell.

Flanagan had a habit of arresting people close to us. I would say she was a passive-aggressive police chief, but her behavior qualified as plain old aggressive. Anyone who'd ever met Germsany Turtle would know immediately that the man was not capable of murder. Apparently Flanagan disagreed.

Flanagan was standing out in front of the police department when Miss May, Teeny, and I pulled up in Miss May's yellow VW bus.

"Good morning, ladies." Chief Flanagan smiled. "Looks like that fog is finally lifting."

Teeny shook her head. "Too bad you got so much fog in your brain. Germany Turtle is less threatening than an actual turtle. Why did you arrest him?"

Flanagan smirked. "Not at liberty to say. Well, I suppose I could tell you. But I don't want to. See, I'm not in the habit of sharing information with meddlesome sleuths. I'm a real cop. I was the star of my rookie class. Then I paid my dues, worked my way up to chief. You'll never get that far by teaming up with bumbling nitwits in your investigations."

Miss May laughed. "You're in a mood."

"I sure am. I'm in a great mood. Finally got the bad guy. He's going away for a long time."

I shook my head. "I'm sorry. Maybe you don't remember who we are. Hey. I'm Chelsea. This is my aunt Miss May and our spunky friend, Teeny. We're actually kind of famous here in Pine Grove. Because we solve murders before the police can. Have you heard of us?"

Flanagan glared at me.

I turned to Miss May and Teeny. "How many murders have we solved now? I've really lost count."

Miss May sighed. "OK, Chelsea. Your boyfriend is in jail so you're upset. But let's show the chief a little respect. She almost solved that last one."

Teeny laughed with a loud snort. "Good one. Oh boy. Legendary one-liner, May. They're going to put that one in the movie they make about your life."

Miss May walked toward the police department entrance. Flanagan blocked her path. "Where do you think you're going?"

"Every prisoner in Pine Grove gets one visit on the day of the arrest. Germany Turtle called us. We're here to visit."

"I can only allow one person in there with him," Flanagan said. "New rule. For safety reasons."

Teeny scoffed. "Safety reasons? Are we talking about the same Germany Turtle? That strange little nerd who studied lions in Africa and thinks sweater vests and cowboy hats are a 'daring combination?'"

Flanagan crossed her arms. "One visitor. That's final."

Miss May shrugged and turned to me. "Looks like you've got a date with Germany," she said. "Try to find out the details of his arrest. I'm sure the police bungled the procedure. We can get him released pretty quickly if they didn't follow protocol. Oh. And see if he has any more information about who might have killed Adam Smith and Zambia."

"It is unlawful for you to pursue this investigation," snapped Flanagan.

"We're not pursuing anything," said Miss May. "I'm just a nosy old lady who runs the apple orchard. And I love to gossip."

Miss May grabbed the door to the police department and held it open for me. I nodded at Flanagan as I entered the lobby. I gave her a little smirk as I entered. Her face reddened so deeply I thought she might explode.

It felt good standing up to Chief Flanagan. Even if she still had the legal authority, we had the upper hand in the battle of wits.

Deputy Hercules let me into a small interrogation room, where Germany sat behind a folding table. His hands were cuffed behind his back. And his ankles were cuffed together too. Several feelings hit me at once. Love, fury, sympathy, sadness. What came out of my mouth was a mangled expression of all of those feelings... Sort of.

"Garf!"

"Excuse me," Hercules said. "Did you just say 'garf?'"

"Yeah, I did," I said. "And what I meant by that was, uh, well, what I meant was, Germany are you OK? Why do they have you cuffed like this?"

I rushed toward Germany and reached out to hug him. Deputy Hercules stepped in my path. "No touching. You have ten minutes. Ten minutes only."

"Good job, Deputy Hercules." Flanagan entered the

room. "I'll supervise this one. Take a break. Drink one of those K-cups you like so much."

Hercules nodded and exited. Flanagan smirked and gestured at a folding chair across from Germany. "Please. Continue."

I went to a folding chair and sat across from Germany. He offered me a weak smile. "Have no fear, Chelsea. Although my wrists and legs are currently bound, my devotion to you is still boundless. My love cannot be confined or contained. Seeing you here gives me strength. The florescent light makes your eyes shine brighter than—"

I held up my hand. "Germany. This is sweet. You're wonderful. But you're eating up our ten minutes and I don't think Chief Flanagan is in a generous mood."

"I'm not," Flanagan said with a big smile.

Germany stammered and side-eyed the chief. "They didn't tell me anything when they arrested me. I was just sitting at home, reading medieval poetry, when the chief showed up and placed me under arrest."

"And they said you were being arrested for the murders of Adam Smith and Zambia Baker?"

Germany nodded. He shot a nervous glance over at Flanagan. "I'm not sure how much I should say with the chief here in the room. I haven't seen many police procedurals on broadcast television, but as far as I recall the prisoner is often advised not to speak without a lawyer present."

I nodded. "That's smart. I don't trust the police in this town. They can't solve any crimes, first of all. And they keep making silly arrests."

"This is not a silly arrest," said Flanagan.

I looked back at her. "You're right. This man is clearly a killer. All killers read medieval love poetry in their spare time. Look at him. He's a brute. Cold-blooded and ruthless."

Germany furrowed his eyebrows. "I hope you're being sarcastic, Chelsea. Although I'm aware that I can be a passionate man and my recent discovery of theater has led me deeper into my emotions... I do not think of myself as a brute. Rather, I think of myself as a flower. A masculine flower, don't get me wrong. But a pretty flower, nonetheless."

Flanagan laughed. I glared at her. "Don't laugh at my flower man." I turned back to Germany. "Of course I don't think you're a brute, Germany. I was being very, very, very, very sarcastic."

Germany breathed a sigh of relief. "Thank goodness."

"I wish I had more information," I said. "I want to get you out of here but it's hard if we can't discuss any details of this case."

Germany stroked his chin. "Something tells me you already have all the information you need. Think about everything you've learned over the past few days. Replay the conversations in your mind. You have all the ingredients for a rich soup. You just have to put all the clues together and see what kind of soup you have." It wasn't the best analogy I'd ever heard, but I didn't interrupt. "You're the smartest woman I've ever known. Teeny and Miss May are likewise brilliant. I'm not worried. I know you're going to get me out of here. Until that time comes, you should not worry either. The jail cell here is comfortable. Made more comfortable by thoughts of you."

I looked down. Germany's confidence in my abilities somehow made me feel insecure. Like I didn't deserve for him to have such faith in me. I looked up and we made eye contact. "You really think I have all the information I need?"

Germany nodded. At that moment I had a thought that changed the course of the investigation. A classic light bulb moment.

Coincidentally, the fluorescent light flickered and went out at that exact second. I gasped.

*Weird.*

"Hercules!" Flanagan called out. "Come change the light bulb in here please! And Chelsea? It's time for you to leave."

## 38

## LIGHT BULB

*M*iss May and Teeny were leaning against the bus waiting for me when I exited the police station. They both stood straight up when I emerged. Miss May walked toward me. "What happened?"

"We have to go back to that junkyard." I crossed straight to the bus and climbed inside. Miss May and Teeny followed behind me.

"Back to the junkyard? For what?" Miss May put the keys in the ignition. "We already confirmed Zambia and Adam were having an affair. She was destroying the evidence from that relationship."

I shook my head. "No. We overlooked something in that dumpster. I barely had time to search it. Wayne arrived. He tried to seduce me."

"Wayne tried to seduce you?" Teeny leaned forward. "You didn't mention that."

"Well not exactly seduce. Whatever. I'm using a short-hand. He interrupted me," I said.

"Wayne is always trying to seduce her." Miss May started

the car. "That junkyard is owned and operated by Zambia's brother. He's not going to let you back in. I still don't understand why we're headed there."

I turned to Miss May with a serious look in my eye. "I have a theory. But you need to be patient. I'll tell you but I want you to take this theory seriously."

Miss May turned up her palms. "OK. What are you thinking?"

Teeny grinned. "It's the Russian spy thing. The two of you always doubt me. But this stuff happens. It's ripped from the headlines."

I turned back to Teeny. "I'm not talking about Russian spies." I looked over at Miss May. "I'm talking about my parents."

Miss May hung her head. "OK. Go on."

"We don't really talk about them. We never have. I understand that. But this whole thing seems intertwined with their deaths."

"You mean because Zambia was so close with your parents when they were alive?"

I nodded. "Kind of, yeah. Because she was mayor back then. I don't know. When I was inside that police station Germany challenged me. He told me we already had all the clues we need. And the way he looked at me... I could tell he meant it. Germany believes we can solve this with the information we currently have. And Zambia's connection to my parents is an important part of that information."

Miss May bit her lower lip. "I suppose."

I shook my head. "No. It is. Think about it. When I went over to Zambia's house this morning it was because I wanted to learn more information about my parents. But she died just before I had a chance to talk to her."

"Someone killed her," said Teeny.

I nodded. "Exactly. What if the killer realized I was getting close to the truth about my parents? This whole thing is connected to the past, I'm almost certain of that. Was Adam Smith in Pine Grove when my parents were killed?"

Miss May scratched her head. "I believe he was, yes. He was still active on Broadway then. But he had a house up here. Came up sometimes when he wasn't in a show."

I smacked my knee. "We have to go back to that junkyard. The two of them knew. Adam and Zambia. They knew what happened to my parents. What if they were the only two who knew the truth other than the killer? I have to at least try to find out."

"Chelsea..." Miss May started.

I suddenly realized I was crying. Silent tears streamed down my cheeks. "Those were my parents. I'm never going to get them back. The least I can do is find out what happened to them."

Miss May put her hand on my arm. We made eye contact. I saw that she was crying too. Then Teeny let out an incredibly loud sob from the back seat.

I turned back. Teeny blew her nose into a handkerchief so vigorously the handkerchief fluttered in the wind. We all laughed.

The laugh was cathartic, therapeutic, cleansing. We laughed for almost a full minute, then we settled down, caught out breath...

"OK," Miss May said. "We're going to go back to that junkyard. We're going to explore this theory."

I wiped my nose. "Just to humor me?"

Miss May shrugged. "Your theory is the best lead we've

got. But Teeny and I and this big yellow bus are too obvious. We can't go back there."

Teeny leaned forward. "I agree. It has to be you. And you're going to need a disguise."

## 39

## BIG DAN'S DISGUISES

"*I* can't do that." Big Dan slid out from underneath the SUV he was working on. "It's the middle of the workday. And I'm terrible with disguises. Haven't dressed up for Halloween since I was seven years old and even then I just tossed a sheet over my head and called myself Big Spooky Dan."

"Were you big when you were seven?" I asked.

"No," Big Dan said. "But people still called me Big Dan."

Miss May shook her head. "Big Dan, you don't have to get dressed up in a disguise. Chelsea would be wearing the disguise."

Big Dan steadied himself on the fender of the vehicle and stood, wiping his hands on his jeans. "So Chelsea is going to have a sheet over her head? That's not going to allow her to penetrate the junkyard undetected. She'll draw attention to herself. I doubt those junkyard boys believe in ghosts. And even if they did, they'll be able to see her sneakers. Nice sneakers, by the way."

I looked down at my plain white shoes. "Thanks. I've always thought they were boring."

Big Dan nodded. "They are. But in a good way. Like watching the news in a language you don't speak or read or understand. Soothing."

Teeny laughed. "You say the weirdest stuff, Big Dan." Teeny got serious. "But we really need you to help us. We need to get Chelsea a good disguise. Then you go to the junkyard and say you're looking for a car door or something."

"Why would I go to the junkyard for a car door? I rarely need doors. And when I do, I go to the auto salvage lot."

Miss May sighed. "So you tell the junkyard boys that you're just coming from the salvage lot and they didn't have the door you need and you're stopping by on the off-chance that they'll have it."

"I need to think this over." Big Dan entered the office adjacent to his garage and popped a K-cup in his little coffee machine. "Who wants coffee? I can only make one cup at a time, so if you all say yes we'll be here all day."

Miss May waved him away. "We're over-caffeinated already."

Teeny nodded. "I'm over-caffeinated when I wake up in the morning. Then I drink coffee and I'm way over-caffeinated. Then around two or three I get a latte with sprinkles and I'm over-sugared and over- caffeinated."

Miss May chuckled. "And you wonder why you can't fall asleep!"

Teeny shook her head. "No. I can't fall asleep because my mind goes too fast. Nothing to do with caffeine."

"You should try one of those rain machines," said Big Dan. "I put mine on the loudest setting. I think it's called 'violent thunderstorm.' Not sure why, but the rolling thunder, the claps of of lightning, and the pounding rain put me right to sleep. I hate rain, don't like getting rained on, but I like it from the machine."

Teeny nodded. "I'll try that. If it works for you, I bet it's great."

Teeny and Big Dan made eye contact. I wasn't sure why those two didn't just go out on a date already. They got along great. They had obvious chemistry. When they were together, conversation flowed freely and easily. Teeny thought Big Dan was the funniest guy in the world. And I was pretty sure he thought she was cute and friendly.

Big Dan pressed a button on the coffee machine and watched his single cup of coffee fill one tiny drip at a time. There was a long, quiet moment.

"By the way, Big Dan," Miss May said. "I don't know if we ever really thanked you. You were basically the hero of our last investigation. That's why we're here. You're kind of the fourth member of our team, Big Dan."

Big Dan looked over at Miss May. "I bet you say that to all the girls."

"We most certainly do not," said Teeny. "These two barely acknowledge my existence on these investigations. I just got anointed the third official member of the detective team, I don't know, a couple murders ago. I'm actually annoyed right now. Big Dan gets to be number four? He's barely around at all."

"I'm not involved often but when I am I make it count." Big Dan took a sip of his coffee. "Yum. Tastes just like the gas station."

Miss May gestured to a few folding chairs that were propped against the wall. "Mind if I take a seat?"

"Sit as long as you want. But I need to get back out there and work on that car. I think I've just about got it fixed. One good, hard kick and it'll be running like brand-new."

Teeny laughed. "Is that the secret of being a mechanic? People bring their cars and you kick them?"

Big Dan nodded. "Sometimes a punch on the hood if it's a tough job. Charge extra for that." Big Dan killed his cup of coffee in one big swig. "OK, ladies. Have a nice day." He began to exit the office. I jumped up and stood in his way.

"Wait."

Big Dan stopped in his tracks. "Chelsea. Almost forgot you were here. These other two talk so much."

"Did you know my parents?" I swallowed. I wasn't sure where I was going with this line of inquiry, but I needed Big Dan's help and I was willing to try anything.

"Sure. I knew 'em. Great people. Worked on their Volvo a couple times."

"Cool," I said. "Did you know that their deaths... might not have been accidental? Miss May has suspected for a long time that they were murdered." Big Dan looked over at Teeny. She shrugged.

Miss May stepped forward. "Chelsea. Maybe we should let Big Dan get back to work."

"That's fine. I just want to know."

Big Dan tossed his cup in the trash. "I've heard that, yes."

"We think the murders we're investigating now might be connected to my parents' deaths. Evidence of their murder is at that junkyard. I can feel it. But it's going to be hard to get in there without you."

I spotted a pair of coveralls that Big Dan had draped over his desk chair. I crossed, grabbed the clothes and held them up. "If I put these on and smear some oil on my face, I can pass as your assistant. We can wait for you to get done working on that car out there. But then we have to get to that junkyard."

Big Dan nodded. "OK. I'll go. But those coveralls belong to Giant John. I might have to give you a smaller size."

I laughed. "Perfect. Thank you."

Big Dan shrugged. "I've always been sorry about what happened to your parents. If I can help solve that mystery... I don't care about fixing up a car right this minute."

I gave Big Dan a small smile. "So you want to go right now?"

Big Dan popped another K-cup in his machine. "Right after my second cup of coffee."

## 40

# JUNKYARD DOGS

"*I*'m Al Baker. I own this junkyard. And I guarantee we don't have any car doors." Zambia's brother, Al aka Junk Boy, crossed his arms and glared. His large frame and deep scowl were intimidating. Al made Big Dan look tiny.

I cowered behind Big Dan. Although I felt fairly inconspicuous in my coveralls, I knew the disguise could have been better so I wanted to remain in the background. Also, let's be honest, I was scared.

Big Dan bit his lower lip. "No car doors. That's a shame." He scanned the junkyard. "Do you have anything car-related? I could use radios. Also wouldn't turn down a nice wheel or two. And everybody in town knows I love bucket seats. Give me a bucket seat and I'll be happy for a month."

Al shook his head. "We mostly clear out people's homes. People don't keep car parts in their homes. You need to go back to the salvage yard."

Big Dan ran his tongue over his teeth. "I thought you might try to send me back to the salvage yard. Those guys are on my bad list. They haven't had a good door in months.

If I show up looking for a good door, don't try to sell me a door with a big ding in it, am I right?"

Al shrugged. "If you don't want a door with a big ding in it, don't try to get it from the salvage lot. Or a junkyard."

"Back in the day you could get high quality goods at junkyards. The word junk used to mean something. These days... It's a disgrace. All you can get in the junkyard is actual junk."

"If you wanted a microwave I could sell you that. I also have plenty of armchairs. Lamps. Boy, do I have lamps. There are at least fifty filing cabinets in one of our storage units. We call that the filing cabinet cabinet. I don't know what else to tell you, man."

Big Dan scrunched up his face. "Let me take a look around. I'll find the car doors."

I winced. Big Dan had gotten caught up on our "car door plan." He needed to be more malleable, but he seemed stuck. I stepped forward and whispered in Big Dan's ear. "No more car door talk. Tell him you're also looking for house-hold goods."

Al narrowed his eyes. "Why doesn't your assistant talk out loud? Is there something up with his brain?"

I bristled. "My brain is in tip-top condition." I spoke in a low, masculine voice. "They wanted me in the Marines."

"They wanted you in the Marines but you chose to be an assistant to a small-town mechanic instead?"

I shrugged. "What can I say? I love fixing cars."

Al rubbed his chin. "You look familiar. Do you have a sister?"

"Forget my assistant," said Big Dan. "I'm not here looking for a door anymore. I need household goods. Show me to the household goods."

I pointed over at Zambia's dumpster. "I bet you there's

some household goods in that one. Looks like it's over-flowing with stuff."

"OK. Explore the lot. Make note of anything you find and I'll quote you a price at the end."

Big Dan nodded. "Thank you. Was that so hard?"

Al shrugged. "It was easy once you stopped fixating on car doors."

Al ambled away, scrolling on his cell phone. Big Dan turned to me and wiped the sweat off his forehead. "That was touch and go for a while. I'm not a good liar."

I rolled my eyes. "You're a terrible liar, Big Dan. That's why you're a great mechanic. It's also why we should never take you on a mission like this again."

Big Dan crossed his arms. "Hey. I got the job done, didn't I?"

I chuckled. "I suppose you did." I pointed at Zambia's dumpster on the far side of the junkyard. "Thank goodness her stuff hasn't been incinerated yet. Come on. Let's see what we can find."

Five minutes later, and Big Dan and I were side-by-side in Zambia's dumpster. The contents of the dumpster were much as I had left them. Random documents, files and folders tossed in every direction, interspersed with random junk from Zambia's house.

I hadn't really envisioned myself climbing around dumpsters so much as an adult woman, but honestly, it was kind of exciting. I could tell Big Dan was having a good time too, sorting through a stranger's junk. Even if there weren't any usable car parts.

Big Dan picked up a broken, empty picture frame. He stuck his head through where the photo should have been. "What are we looking for again?"

I exhaled. "I'm not sure." I kicked an old shoebox aside.

"Look for stuff that seems old. My parents died over twenty years ago so if there's evidence of their murder in this dumpster it's going to be at least twenty years old."

"I feel a little bad, digging through a dead woman's dumpster," Big Dan said. "It feels wrong. Like trespassing or something."

"There's that trademark honesty again. But you shouldn't think of it as trespassing. Instead, think of this like our research expedition. We're hunting for information. And whatever we find might stop someone else from getting murdered. What better way to honor someone's life than to use their belongings to save another life?"

Big Dan nodded and continued sifting through Zambia's junk. He pushed aside a lamp. He turned over an end table. He sifted through a binder, one page at a time.

After a few minutes, Big Dan called me over to another section of the dumpster. "Look at this."

I slowly stepped over to Big Dan. He tilted a box toward me so I could see inside. "Old videocassettes. I bet these are worth a lot of money online. Some rare Disney movies in here. Plus a lot of musicals. That's fun."

"That's why you called me over?"

Big Dan shrugged. "You're a millennial. Thought you'd appreciate the nostalgia."

I took a closer look inside the box. Most of the tapes were unimportant but then one caught my eye. It was a VHS copy of the movie production of *West Side Story.*

I reached into the box and pulled the movie out. "That's strange."

Big Dan looked over at me. "What?"

"Every single video in this box looks like it's been watched a hundred times. The covers are wrinkled and white. The images have been rubbed off the front. Zambia clearly watched these movies."

Big Dan shrugged. "So?"

I held up a copy of *West Side Story*. "This movie is in pristine condition. Like it's never been watched. Or even touched." I carefully opened the plastic case and pulled out the videocassettes "And this video isn't a copy of *West Side Story*. It's not labeled at all."

Big Dan leaned over to get a closer look. "That is strange. Zambia took such care with this collection. It's incredibly organized. It's odd that this one, which seems to be in mint condition, contains the wrong movie."

"We need to find out was on this tape," I said. "Do you have a VCR?"

Big Dan shook his head.

I swallowed. "Then let's go find one."

## 41

## BE KIND, REWIND

*I* had no idea it would be so hard to find a VCR in modern-day America.

The Internet was king of TV and movie viewing. Even DVD players were old-fashioned. Almost no one preferred to watch videocassettes for entertainment. So it was much more challenging than anticipated to watch that tape Big Dan and I found in the dumpster that day.

After we left the junkyard, I went straight to *Grandma's* to ask Teeny if she had a VCR we could use. Teeny laughed in my face before I finished asking the question.

"Come on, Chelsea. I told you. I'm not old. I'm hip. I watch movies on my phone while I'm using the bathroom. I don't have a VCR anymore. Tossed that thing in the trash at least six months ago."

I didn't have any luck with Miss May, either. She didn't laugh in my face but she did doubt the promise of the VHS I had found.

"I'm confused," she said. "You think this videotape is important just because the box was in perfect shape? I see the logic, kind of, but it's not very promising. Did you find anything else in the dumpster?"

"No," I said. "But I'm telling you, this tape is something."

I went to the electronic store in town and the kid who worked there didn't even know what I was talking about. "What's a VCR?" He asked. "Does that stand for something?"

I groaned. "You work at an electronic store and you don't even know what a VCR is?"

The kid rolled his eyes. "There's always somebody coming in here, asking for old stuff. Tape players? Eight tracks? Radios? What the heck is a radio? I haven't heard of like, any of that ancient crap. Sorry."

I opened my mouth to respond, but I could tell I wasn't going to be able to connect with this kid on technological issues. So I just thanked him for his time and left.

I pounded the pavement for hours, asking everyone I knew if they could help me find a way to play the video tape. No one could help. So I went back to the farmhouse to eat dinner with KP and Miss May.

Miss May had made split pea soup for dinner that night. She already had three bowls out on the big, wooden kitchen table when I got home. She also had a nice container of Parmesan set aside. And there was a big crust of Italian bread in the center of the table.

KP threw up his hands when I entered. "Finally. We've been waiting here for ten minutes. My peas are going to get cold. I fed See-Saw her dinner. Then I had to watch the little limpy dog eat his dog food. That made me jealous. Then this new kitty-cat you brought home ate her dinner. Everyone got to eat except old KP. Wash up. I'm sick of waiting."

I laughed. "Hi KP. Nice to see you, too."

"Yeah. Yeah. I been working on the peach trees all day. I'm a little agitated. Gotta get those peaches ready for summertime. They're our best seller of the season. Wanna make sure we have a strong crop."

"You can make sure of something like that?" I asked. "It's only March."

KP shook his head. "No you cannot make sure of something like that. That's why I've been so frustrated."

"Tell me about it," I said. "I've been looking all over town for a working VCR and people keep laughing in my face."

KP laughed.

"Yes. Exactly like that. Doesn't feel too good."

I washed my hands in the farmhouse sink and dried them on a plaid dishtowel. Then Miss May and I joined KP at the dinner table. KP grabbed his spoon but Miss May held up her hand before he had a chance to eat. "Hold on. Sorry. We need to pray."

Miss May didn't always pray before meals, at least not out loud. She was a pragmatic woman, not often prone to expressions of spirituality. But sometimes when she was feeling stressed or worried, she liked to take the time to express gratitude and concern and remind herself not to play God — that was, after all, a task best left to God.

KP lowered his spoon with a grunt. "I already prayed. I prayed and prayed that Chelsea would walk through the door so I could eat dinner. It came true. Hallelujah, amen."

Miss May laughed. "Dear God, thank you for this food. Please look out for the Baker family, and the Smiths as well. Let us have the patience to solve this mystery before anyone else gets harmed. Look out for everyone we love who has passed and everyone who is still with us. Thank you for this great company."

"And look out for my peaches," said KP.

Miss May smiled. "Chelsea. Anything else to add?"

"A VCR would be nice." Someone knocked on the back door three times. The door frame rattled and a male voice rang out. "Chelsea. Miss May. You in there? I heard you need a VCR."

My eyes widened. *Talk about the power of prayer.*

"Who's there?" Miss May called over her shoulder.

Tom Gigley rushed into the kitchen holding a dusty cardboard box. "Smells good in here."

I jumped to my feet. "Tom. You have a VCR in there?"

Tom nodded. "Yup."

I bit my nails. "I bet it's pretty old. Do you think it works?"

Tom nodded. "I know it works. I watched all three *Diehard* movies on this puppy last night. I love my VCR. Don't like the Internet. Don't like the discs. VCR is the best technology ever invented. Can you believe they don't sell them at *J-Mart* anymore?"

I smiled. "I can't believe it, no."

Tom set the box on the table with a sigh. "What are we watching, anyway?"

I grabbed the VHS from the counter and held up. "I don't know. But we're about to find out."

## 42

# CAUGHT ON TAPE

"What kind of popcorn do we want? I found butter, real butter, extra butter, and cheddar." Teeny held up four bags of popcorn and smiled. "I vote for extra butter. Actually, cheddar. No, you know what? Both."

"I'm too nervous to eat," I said.

Miss May turned back to Teeny. "I'm too nervous not to eat. I'll take cheddar."

Tom poked his head up from behind the television where he had been setting up the VCR. "Cheddar sounds good to me. Also, extra butter. And can you put butter on the cheddar?"

Teeny pointed at Tom. "I like the way you think. Not heart-healthy but this is a special occasion. We're about to find the killer."

"Or Zambia's home movies of a vacation to Hawaii," I said. "Who knows what's on this tape?" On the inside, I thought that the tape was probably the key to our investigation, but I wanted to keep expectations low.

"We're not watching anything if I can't get this VCR set

up," Gigley said. "Things weren't so complicated before God invented the Internet."

I laughed. "I remember when I was a kid everything had to have wires. Wires, wires, everywhere. Now we live in a wireless world, which seems like it should make things easier but—"

"But nooo," Gigley said.

Miss May shrugged. "A lot of times they say wireless but there are still a lot of wires involved. I don't understand that. If you say wireless, I don't want any wires. I hate when things get tangled and dusty. I don't like dealing with plugging things in."

Tom groaned from behind the TV. "Then you most certainly should not look back here. Good thing I'm not in charge of defusing a bomb because we would have all exploded by now."

"The stakes are just as high," I said. "This tape might unlock our investigation and stop a murderer from killing again. Time is of the essence. You should take this seriously, Tom." *Low expectations, out the window.*

"I am." Tom's voice was stern. "I'm doing my best. Let me focus."

I took a step back. "Sorry. I know you're just trying to help. And you're the only way we can access a VCR without a time machine so I should be more appreciative."

Tom grumbled. "I can think of a long list of reasons why you should be more appreciative."

Teeny reentered holding a smoking, tar-black bag of popcorn. "Extra butter is off the menu this evening. So sorry, ladies and gentlemen. There was an accident in the kitchen. But cheddar is on its way."

Miss May shook her head. "You own an incredible

restaurant yet you can't make a bag of popcorn. How is that possible?"

"Popcorn is not on the menu at *Grandma's*. And never will be. We don't own a single microwave in the restaurant. Everything is made fresh."

"That's why I love that place." Tom gave Teeny a thumbs-up from behind the television.

"And that's why I love you, Tom." Teeny hurried back toward the kitchen. "Back with cheddar in thirty seconds."

Teeny's footsteps padded down the hall toward the kitchen. After five or ten seconds she called back. "Nevermind. Cheddar's a no-go."

Miss May chuckled. "Forget the popcorn. Come back in here. Almost ready."

Tom crawled out from behind the TV and turned it on. "I did it. The VCR is set up."

Teeny darted back into the room, face pale. She bit her nails. "So it's time to watch the tape?"

Tom nodded. He grabbed the tape from the table and slid it into the VCR. There were a few seconds of black and white static than the tape began to play... And it was not a vacation to Hawaii.

It was security camera footage. Grainy and a little difficult to see. The footage was from a parking lot. There was one car in the parking lot, parked beneath a tall light post. There were no people in the image. Just the car and the light and... *There had to be something else, right?*

Miss May furrowed her brow. "This looks old."

I nodded. "Definitely not *West Side Story.*"

Miss May looked over at me. We made eye contact. I had a feeling we were on the cusp of something big. But so far, there was no movement.

Then a dark figure crossed into the frame and

approached the car. Miss May leaned toward the television set. "Who is that?"

Teeny shrugged. She shoved a handful of burnt popcorn in her mouth. "I can't tell."

"How are you eating that popcorn?" I asked. "It smells like the bottom of a fireplace."

"I like it burned."

Tom pointed at the TV screen. "The guy's going underneath the car."

Indeed, the dark figure was on his back under the hood of the car, tampering. I suddenly remembered that we were watching footage that might be related to my parents' death. They had died in a car accident. Faulty brakes.

I drew in a sharp breath. "Is that... Is that a Volvo?"

Miss May got closer to the screen, squinting. Then she turned back and nodded. "I'm almost positive that's your parents' car. This... This video must have been taken that night."

"That guy, whoever he is...he's doing something shady!"

I scooted up to the edge of my seat. I felt compelled to see every detail of the video. I didn't want to watch, but I also couldn't look away. Then...the video ended. The screen cut back to the black and white static.

"No. That can't be all there is. We need to keep watching."

"Let me fast-forward." Tom pressed fast-forward on the VCR. There was nothing but black and white fuzz for the duration of the tape.

I put my head in my hands. "This is terrible. That's a video that shows someone tampering with my parents' car the night they died. But we can't tell who it is. We can't tell anything from that video."

"Hold on a second," said Miss May. "Zambia would not

have held onto this video for so many years if it didn't prove something. She wouldn't have tried to destroy it at the junkyard. And she wouldn't have been killed by someone who wanted to keep this video a secret."

Teeny nodded and crunched on more popcorn. "Miss May is right. Let's watch it again."

Tom looked over at me. "Again?"

I nodded.

"Are you sure?" Tom's finger hovered over the play button.

"I'm sure. Play it."

Seconds later, we were back at the beginning of the video. The street light. The lone car in the parking lot. The dark figure approaching.

"Can you tell who it is?" Teeny asked.

"The face is invisible," said Miss May. "But hang on a second." Miss May rubbed her chin. "Tom. Rewind back to the beginning."

Tom hit rewind then pressed play again. The car in an empty parking lot. The dark figure approaching the vehicle. Miss May pointed at the TV. "Look. We don't need to see that guy's face. The evidence is in the way he walks. See how he kind of toddles, dragging his right foot behind him?"

I took a closer look. Miss May was right. The figure in the television set seem to have a very slight limp. "I see that. Yeah."

Miss May let out a long, deep breath. "Do you recognize that walk?"

I suddenly remembered the bannister on Zambia's stairs. How loose and wobbly it had been — as if someone had been heavily leaning on it. Like someone with a limp.

I gasped. "Oh my god. I know who killed my parents! And Adam and Zambia!"

Miss May stood and pulled on her coat. "Let's go find them."

## 43

## FOR PETE'S SAKE

"Everyone stop asking questions. I need to focus on my driving." Miss May hung a sharp left and hurtled down Whitehill Road, headed toward *Peter's Land and Sea*.

"But hold on. Jefferson Nebraska can't be the killer," I said. "He was at the restaurant when Adam Smith was killed. Remember? He's the one who served Dorothy after she stormed out of the performance."

"I don't know about any of that." Miss May blew through a red light.

"Slow down," said Teeny. "That was a red light."

"We're fine." Miss May took another hard left turn. "There were no cars. And we need to get where we're going. Fast."

"I'm with Chelsea," said Tom from the backseat. "If Jefferson had an alibi for Adam's murder why are you in such a hurry to get to him?"

"Because he's the only man I've ever known with a limp like that. I'm almost positive he's the one in that security footage."

I bit my lip. "And Jefferson definitely lived here when my parents died?"

Miss May glanced at me out of the corner of her eye. "Yes. He used to sort of have a crush on your mother, in fact. Then he took off on his motorcycle less than a week after they passed."

"That rat." Teeny clenched her little fists. "That disgraceful, despicable rat."

"The guy seems like a rat," said Tom. "I agree. But I'm hung up on the alibi. If he was at the restaurant that night he couldn't have killed Adam. And if he didn't kill Adam, there's no good reason to connect him to Zambia's murder."

"Jefferson said he was at the restaurant that night," said Miss May. "When he told us that, we had no reason not to trust in. But we never confirmed the alibi."

My chest tightened. "You're right. We took his word for it."

Miss May looked at me. "That's why we're going back to the restaurant now. To find out if he was telling the truth."

A few minutes later, Miss May burst into *Peter's Land and Sea*. Teeny, Tom, and I followed, all panting and struggling to keep up. Miss May walked with strong determination. She charged straight up to the hostess. "Is Jefferson Nebraska working?"

The hostess shook her head. "He's off tonight."

"Where's Petey?"

The hostess stammered. Miss May pushed passed her and strode into the dining room. She looked around with her hands on her hips. "Petey. Where is Petey?"

Restaurant patrons looked at one another, confused. An older man wiped his mouth and pointed toward the kitchen. "I believe I saw him go that way. He didn't look happy."

Miss May nodded. "Thank you." She turned and

addressed the crowded room of diners. "Sorry for the interruption everyone. Enjoy your meals."

Miss May hurried toward the kitchen. We all followed.

Tom turned to me and Teeny. "This is exciting."

Teeny nodded. "Get ready, Tommy boy. The excitement has only just begun."

The kitchen at *Peter's Land and Sea* was chaotic. A line of chefs chopped and sautéed and plated furiously. Waiters crossed back and forth at top speed. The head chef, a bearded man with lots of tattoos, barked orders from the stove. The place felt like a warship in the middle of a battle. But the general, Petey, was nowhere to be seen.

Miss May shook her head. "This place is a madhouse."

Teeny smiled. "I taught Petey well. This kitchen is running like a well-oiled machine. No wonder this restaurant does so much business."

Miss May scanned the kitchen. She wiped sweat from her brow. "Hello? Is Petey back here? For Pete's sake, where is that boy?"

I giggled. Miss May glared at me. "Don't even, Chelsea. Now's not the time for wordplay."

A chef looked over at us. "Miss May. You need to leave. Working kitchen."

Miss May waved the chef away. "Shove it, kid. This is important."

"They're fine." Petey approached holding a large box of produce. He put the box on the counter. The cooks descended on the produce and the box was empty within seconds. *Like hungry vultures*, I thought. Petey turned to us. "I presume you're here about the investigation. Let's try to make it quick. Dinner rush."

"No problem," said Miss May. "I've got one question for you."

Petey shrugged. "Go ahead."

"Was Jefferson Nebraska working here last Friday at the time of Adam Smith's murder?"

## 44

## KUNG PAO MURDER

"I knew it." Miss May jumped in the van and started it with a scowl. "I knew Jefferson Nebraska was lying about working that night."

I jumped into the passenger seat and buckled my seatbelt. "But if Jefferson was lying that means Dorothy might've been lying, too. He was her alibi."

Teeny nodded. "And Dorothy had plenty of motive."

"That's why we're going to talk to Jefferson right now." Miss May did a three-point turn and headed toward town.

"Oh." Tom furrowed his brow. "Perhaps you could drop me at my office first. I've enjoyed the excitement so far. But I don't want to be around any actual murderers. That's dark. And scary."

"You're a lawyer," said Teeny. "Don't you deal with scary stuff all the time?"

"Less than you would think. Mostly I handle estates. Divorces. When Mrs. Harrington fell at the *Shop and Go*, I helped her sue. That kind of stuff is my bread and butter. Not so much homicide."

"Are you sure you want to go back to your office, Tom?" Teeny asked. "It's starting to smell."

Tom narrowed his eyes. "What's starting to smell?"

"Pine Grove is starting to smell," Teeny said. "Like the truth. That means we're getting close."

"As tempting as that sounds, I'd love it if you could drop me off. I'll smell the truth from the comfort of my armchair. I think I'll smell some whiskey at the same time."

Miss May turned to Tom. "I thought you were a dirty martini guy?"

"I've been getting into whiskey lately. Martinis are too much work. Whiskey, I just pour in the glass, add a splash of water, good to go."

Miss May nodded. "I like that efficiency. Now get out."

Miss May slammed to a halt outside Tom's office.

Tom stood. "Oh. That was abrupt. Just like that... I have to leave the van?"

Miss May sighed. "Sorry. Thank you for your help with the VCR. Enjoy your whiskey. We'll let you know what happens."

Tom looked at Miss May with puppy dog eyes. "Am I the fourth official member of the team?"

Miss May smiled. "Fifth. And you're still in your probationary period. Now get out, Tom."

Two minutes later, Miss May parked outside the little Chinese restaurant in the center of town. *China Palace* was in a strip mall, next to an Irish pub and a couple of other local businesses. Jefferson lived in a small apartment above the restaurant. And his light was on.

"Looks like he's home," said Teeny. "Hopefully he's not killing anyone up there."

Miss May shook her head. "Don't say things like that."

Teeny huffed. "Sorry."

I looked the building up and down. "How are we going to get in there?"

Miss May smirked at me. "Mr. G owes me a favor." She entered *China Palace* with a confident stride. Teeny and I trotted along behind her, as we always did.

Mr. G's restaurant was less of a restaurant and more of a counter where people could walk in and order food to go. Mr. G was short and skinny. He always wore a big smile, and his face was on every bag and to-go container in the joint.

"Miss May. Don't tell me. Someone was murdered. And the killer snuck poison into my food. So you think I did it. I've been waiting for this moment," Mr. G said. "Let's go. Interrogate me."

"Not today." Miss May leaned on the counter. "I need to cash in that favor, Mr. G."

Mr. G shrugged. "Which favor? I owe you fifty or sixty. You drove my kids to school. You helped me fix a flat tire. You leave me great reviews for restaurant online."

"I need to cash all of them in right now."

Mr. G's eyes widened. "So you are here about an investigation."

About one minute later, Mr. G unlocked a door in the back of the restaurant. The door led to a rickety old staircase. And the staircase led to Jefferson Nebraska's apartment.

Miss May led the way up the stairs. Like every staircase in every old building in all of Pine Grove, each step protested our weight with a loud creak.

I wiped my sweaty palms on my jeans. I wiped my sweaty forehead on my arm. I belched. "Does anyone else feel really nervous right now?"

Miss May paused and looked back at me. "We're going to be OK. We're just here to talk. And we've done this before."

I nodded. "OK."

Miss May knocked on Jefferson's door three times. Bang. Bang. Bang. "Jefferson. Are you home?"

No answer.

Teeny joined Miss May on the top step. "Maybe we should try to pick the lock. See if we can find any clues in—"

The door opened. There stood Jefferson Nebraska, arms crossed. He scowled. "Miss May. What are you doing here?"

Miss May smiled. "I was hoping we could talk." She pulled a pie from her purse. "I brought apple pie."

"Sure. Come on in."

Jefferson stepped aside and gestured for us to enter. Miss May and I exchanged a concerned look, like, that was a little too easy. Then we walked into Jefferson's apartment. Teeny followed. As soon as the three of us were inside, Jefferson closed the door and locked it.

"Sit on the couch." None of us moved. Jefferson pulled a gun from his waist and pointed at us. "Let me rephrase. Sit. Now."

Miss May looked over at me and Teeny. "Let's do as he says, girls." I plopped down on the center seat of the couch. Miss May and Teeny sat on either side of me.

Jefferson laughed. "You three think you're so powerful. You think you can solve every murder. But who's powerful now? I say sit and you sit. You think you caught me? You think I was just an unsuspecting idiot? No. I've been waiting for you. And I've got it all planned out."

I swallowed. "You have what all planned out?"

Jefferson laughed once more. Then he got serious. "Officer. I'm so glad you're here. Those amateur detectives showed up at my house. The young one tried to hurt me with her ridiculous karate. I was lucky I got to the gun in time. They were trying to kill me! They went crazy with power. They accused me of murder and they wanted me dead and I had to defend myself."

Miss May shook her head. "You think the cops are going to buy that?" She reached into her purse, pulled out the videotape and placed it on the counter. "I know what you did to my sister and my brother-in-law."

I looked down, hands suddenly trembling with rage. "You killed my parents."

Jefferson turned and pointed the gun at me. "I'm sorry."

"You're not even going to deny it?" I demanded.

"I can't. You're right, I did it," Jefferson said. "I wasn't thinking straight. I was in love with your mother, and the jealousy drove me insane. I just... I didn't even really mean to kill them. I was just so angry. I felt bad, afterwards. Of course I felt bed. I left town forever. But I got tired of wandering. I figured enough time had passed—"

Teeny glowered at Jefferson. "So you came back and Zambia threatened to expose you. And she told Adam about what you did. So you had to kill them too."

Jefferson scoffed. "No wonder you're just the assistant detective. That's not how it happened at all."

"So how did it happen?" Miss May asked.

Jefferson removed the safety from the gun. "I didn't want Zambia or Adam dead. But Dorothy knew all about my past crimes. That crazy lady had snooped through Zambia's entire house looking for evidence of the affair, and Dorothy had found the videotape. So she threatened to expose me and what I'd done all those years ago...unless I killed Adam. Once Adam was dead, Zambia got suspicious of me. She was sure I'd killed the man she loved. So she demanded a meeting, then she accused me of killing Adam and told me she was going to the police with everything... So I had no choice. I had to kill her. Just like I have to kill you now."

"What I don't understand," Miss May said, "is why Zambia protected you for all those years. She had proof that you'd committed murder. That you'd murdered two of her closest friends, in fact."

"I had proof that she'd stolen money from the town after she was elected mayor," Jefferson said. "Yeah, sure, she was close to Chelsea's parents, but she'd stolen from them too — taken some of their personal donations to her campaign and used it for her own selfish purposes. She'd stolen and pilfered and cheated her way to the top, and I knew all about it. So we kept each other's secrets. Mutually assured destruction, you know? It worked out for a long time, until it didn't anymore."

"You stupid, lying, murdering—" I stood, my fists balled, but Miss May put a hand on my arm.

"Chelsea."

I sat back down. Jefferson toggled the gun among the three of us. "So tell me... Which one of you wants to die first?"

I looked Jefferson in the eye. That man had killed my parents. He wanted to kill me, too.

I stood again. "Kill me first. Go ahead."

Jefferson shook out his hands to try to steady his nerves. He looked away. And in that moment, I lunged at him. And with all my might, I kicked him...right in his bad leg. Jefferson yelped like a wounded coyote.

I wasn't scared, like I normally was when faced with a killer. I felt invincible. Because I was flooded with a righteous confidence, a gut-wrenching, blinding fury that completely took over my senses. I had no hesitation, no consideration of the consequences. I just wanted to hurt Jefferson Nebraska.

Jefferson tried to get back to his feet, but he was in

obvious pain. He clutched his bad leg and screamed. With tremendous effort, he hoisted himself up, took one heavy step toward me, then another... But the floors in the old, rundown apartment were so crummy that when Jefferson took that second step, he fell through the floorboards and dangled there from his elbows.

Jefferson screamed, even louder this time, and his gun skittered across the floor. I could smell the Chinese food wafting up from the new hole in the floor.

"I'm falling through. Help! I'm falling through."

Miss May climbed to her feet. "You're not falling. You're just stuck."

"Please," Jefferson begged. "I'm sorry. Don't kill me. Are you going to kill me for what I did?"

A female voice rang out from the doorway. "They might not kill you, but I will."

We turned toward the direction of the voice. Dorothy stood in the doorway. She was holding a gun.

## 45

## CONVERTIBLE CHAOS

*J* didn't want Dorothy to shoot anyone. That was the only thought going through my mind as I strode toward her, my hands raised. "Put the gun down," I said.

Dorothy kneed me in the stomach and pushed me away. She held the gun to my head, just inches from my skull. "Sit on the couch. Next to the old ladies."

"Hey. You're older than us," said Teeny. "Just because you have good cheekbones doesn't mean—"

"Sit. Go." Dorothy nudged the gun into my head. I took a step toward the couch, then I spun around and karate kicked Dorothy in the torso. She stumbled back and hit the wall with a loud thud.

But the gun was still in her hand.

Bang! The gun went off. I ducked, the sound reverberating in my ears. I had no idea where the bullet had gone.

Teeny and Miss May shrieked. Jefferson screamed at the top of his lungs.

Dorothy covered her mouth. "Oh my goodness. Oh my goodness. There are bullets in there."

I threw up my hands. "You didn't even think that thing was loaded?"

Dorothy stammered for a few seconds, then she turned and darted out of the apartment, back down the stairs.

My eyes widened. "She's running away. She left."

Teeny and Miss May jumped off the couch. "Don't let her get away. Let's go."

We hurried down the steps, one loud creak at a time. I could hear Jefferson shouting from upstairs as we exited. "Wait. You can't leave me here. I'm stuck."

Miss May made eye contact with Mr. G as we left. "Call the cops."

Mr. G nodded. "Already did."

Dorothy peeled out of the parking lot in an old, white convertible. We followed in our VW bus.

"Go faster." Teeny tapped Miss May's arm. "She's getting away."

"I'm going as fast as I can." Miss May swatted Teeny away. "That convertible is too powerful for us."

"We shoulda taken my car," Teeny said.

Dorothy turned off the main road and followed a sign for the highway.

I leaned forward. "She's leaving town."

Miss May tailed Dorothy toward the highway. "If she gets out on the highway before us, we're not gonna be able to catch up with her."

Teeny bit her nails. "Mr. G said he called the cops. Maybe they'll cut her off."

Miss May shook her head. "I don't think so. They're probably all headed to the *China Palace*. Mr. G might not even know that there's another party involved in this."

I grabbed my phone. "Then I'll call the police. Let them know."

Miss May shrugged. "That's fine. But it's still best if we can catch her now. The cops are gonna take a while to respond."

Ahead, Dorothy got stuck behind a school bus. I pointed. "She slowed down. This is our chance."

Miss May pressed her foot all the way down. The school bus turned down another road and cleared the path for Dorothy. We pulled up beside her just as she began to gain speed once more. Miss May rolled down her window. "Stop the car, Dorothy. The police are on their way."

Dorothy did not look over. She was focused on the road and determined to get away.

"I have to stop her," I said.

Miss May looked back at me. "How?"

"Stay steady. Try to stay side-by-side with her car for a few more seconds."

I stood up out of my seat and opened the sliding door in the side of the van.

Teeny gaped at me. "Chelsea. No."

"We don't have a choice." I looked out. We were neck and neck with Dorothy's car. I crept over to the open door and steadied myself. "I'm going to jump."

"Hurry," said Teeny. "She's putting the top up."

The automatic top to Dorothy's convertible slowly closed. I took a deep breath, shut my eyes, and jumped.

Thwump. I landed in the backseat of Dorothy's car. She swerved and I climbed into the front seat.

"Stop the car."

Dorothy reached under her seat and pulled out a tiny handgun. She pointed the small revolver at me while keeping her eyes on the road. "No. You're my hostage now."

I cringed. I should have thought through my plan more

carefully. I didn't assume Dorothy would have more than one firearm.

Dorothy looked over at me. "Sorry about what happened to your parents. But I'm not going to jail for what I did. I didn't even kill anyone, really. I just suggested it! Suggesting murder is not the same as murder. And I won't let you stop me from making my escape."

Miss May honked the horn on the van, long and loud. She honked again and again.

Dorothy and I were locked in intense eye contact. Like a high stakes staring contest. Two women, ready to fight to the death.

Then...

Crash. I lunged forward in my seat. The car stopped. I hit my head on the windshield.

My vision got blurry. I touched my head and looked at my hand. I was bleeding. I looked over at Dorothy. She was slumped against the wheel.

Then my vision faded and everything went black.

Twenty minutes later, I slowly awoke. Sirens flashed around me. My head had been bandaged. Detective Wayne Hudson stood above me.

He gave me a small smile. "Chelsea. You were in an accident."

Groggy, I propped myself up on one elbow. "Dorothy..."

Wayne nodded. "Teeny and Miss May told us. She's been placed under arrest for conspiracy to commit murder."

I looked around. EMT personnel crouched beside me. I was in the back of an ambulance, parked beside Dorothy's mangled convertible.

"Jefferson Nebraska..." I croaked.

"He's also been placed under arrest for multiple counts of homicide. Although he's not back at the department yet.

Still stuck in the floor above the Chinese place, getting cut out."

I smirked. Despite the circumstances, the image of Jefferson dangling in that apartment was funny. Wayne and I made eye contact. He put his hand on my hand. "I'm glad you're alright."

"Me too."

"Heard you jumped into a moving convertible. That was being driven by an armed criminal."

I moaned. "Should have had a better plan."

Miss May and Teeny approached the back of the ambulance. "Thank goodness, you're awake!" Miss May said.

Wayne nodded a cordial hello, then he took Miss May's hand and helped her to the back of the ambulance. She collapsed on top of me and gave me a big hug. "Chelsea. You scared me."

Teeny flopped on top of Miss May. "Group hug!" Teeny declared.

I laughed. We all did. "I'm going to leave you three to talk." Wayne climbed out of the ambulance, then turned back to me. "Good work, Chelsea."

I smiled. "Thanks."

## 46

## IN SICKNESS AND IN STEALTH

*I*'ve always hated hospitals. My whole life, the only reason I've ever been to one is to visit a sick person. Or a dead person. Or sick person who was about to be dead. So I protested when the ambulance driver told me we were headed to New York Presbyterian. I just wanted to go home. And I insisted that I was fine.

Apparently, medical professionals don't let you go home if you've suffered a broken wrist and a concussion in a car accident. So I lost that argument and had to spend the afternoon in a hospital bed.

Miss May and Teeny hung out with me for most of the day. Then they slipped out to grab some coffee from the break room. And I got a special, surprise visitor.

"Knock, knock." Germany entered, holding flowers.

I smiled the brightest smile in the history of smiles. "Germany. You're out of jail. I've been asking about you."

"Discharge paperwork took a while. I'm not sure the Pine Grove Police Department has ever had to discharge a suspected murderer on the same day they've also arrested two new murderers before. It was a little chaotic."

Germany handed me the flowers. It was the biggest bouquet I'd ever seen, and that was saying something considering that Germany's signature style was giant bouquets. I laughed. "Thank you. Where'd you get so many flowers?"

"I bought every bouquet from the flower shop and had them all combined into one. I wanted the flowers to reflect the depths of my feelings for you, but please, consider this only a fraction of my love. All the flowers in the world wouldn't be enough to demonstrate how relieved I am that you've only suffered a broken bone and a mild concussion from your escapades out on the streets this afternoon."

"I don't have any flowers for you," I said.

"That makes sense, considering the aforementioned concussion and broken bone."

"True," I said. "I suppose I won't feel too bad about it. I'm glad you made it out of jail. Although I'll admit, I liked having a bad boy for a boyfriend. Just for a minute."

Germany stood tall and gave me his best bad boy glare. "Oh, I'm bad. So bad. The type of guy that recycles plastic that still has food particles on it."

I smiled and gestured to a nearby chair. "Pull up a seat. I'll give you a bite of my Jell-O."

"That sounds nice." Germany sat beside me. "Everyone in town is talking about you, by the way. They were all already impressed by you, but now that you've jumped from one car to another... You're a legend. I'm proud of you."

"Thank you."

Germany took my hand. "And is it true... You've solved the mystery of what happened to your parents?"

I nodded. "In a strange way, it makes me sad... Closing that chapter. But I feel more complete. Somehow I feel more...at peace."

"You've gotten closure."

I shrugged. "I'm not sure I'll ever feel closure about my parents. But I did get one step closer."

"That's exactly how I felt when you solved the mystery of my parents' murder," said Germany. "I'm grateful that you know the feeling now. I understand how it's painful. But it's a good pain, and it lessens over time. I'm sorry I couldn't help more, but alas, I was behind bars."

"That's OK, Germany. You helped in your own way."

Germany looked down. He fiddled with the edge of my blanket. "Chelsea?"

I looked up and we made eye contact. "Yes?"

"Perhaps now isn't the time... But a day or two ago... I told you I love you."

"I remember." I laughed.

Germany bit his lower lip. "And?"

I squeezed his hand. Maybe it was my recent near-death experience, or the flood of relief I felt about my parents. Or maybe it was just...love. Whatever it was, I looked into Germany's eyes and I was overcome with feeling. "I love you, too."

Germany leaned over the edge of the bed and kissed me. The kiss was...relaxing. It grounded me in the moment, and I let it wash over me, like a warm bath.

"Good kiss," he said.

I nodded. "I agree."

Miss May crept into the room on her tippy toes. "Guys?"

Germany and I turned toward her. "Yeah?" I said.

"Sorry to interrupt," said Miss May. "But the whole town is here to see you."

I sat up. "They are?"

Miss May smiled. She crossed to the curtain hiding my bed from view and pulled it back. There stood at least half of the population of Pine Grove. They exploded with applause when they saw me. I laughed.

"Everybody wanted to celebrate the ending of another mystery but we couldn't do it without you," said Miss May. "Should I tell them to come in?"

I smiled. "Of course. Let's party. There's plenty of Jell-O to go around."

The End

Dear Reader,

Thank you for joining Chelsea, Teeny and Miss May on this wild ride!

I hope you enjoyed this book and had fun trying to solve the mystery right alongside the girls.

The next book in this series is called *Peaches and Scream*.

You'll love this cozy because it's got a tough mystery and plenty of laughs. And you won't believe what happens next!

Search *Peaches and Scream* on Amazon to grab your copy now.

Thanks!
Chelsea

Made in United States
North Haven, CT
29 May 2023

37127862R00146